PENGUIN BOOKS

# MORE TALES OF THE UNEXPECTED

Roald Dahl's parents were Norwegian, but he was born in Llandaff, Glamorgan, in 1916, and educated at Repton School. On the outbreak of World War II, he enlisted in the R.A.F. at Nairobi. He was severely wounded after joining a fighter squadron in Libya, but later saw service as a fighter pilot in Greece and Syria. In 1942 he went to Washington as Assistant Air Attaché and it was there he started to write short stories. Later he was transferred into Intelligence and ended the war as a Wing Commander. His first twelve short stories, based on his wartime experiences, were originally published in leading American magazines and later as a book, *Over to You*. His short stories, which have received extraordinary acclaim, have been translated into many languages and have been bestsellers all over the world. The books in which they are collected are *Someone Like You*, *Kiss Kiss*, *Twenty-Nine Kisses from Roald Dahl*, *Switch Bitch* and *Ah! Sweet Mystery of Life*. Anglia Television dramatized a selection of these short stories, which are published in Penguin as *Tales of the Unexpected* and *More Tales of the Unexpected*. His other publications include his highly praised novel, *My Uncle Oswald*, a collection of his finest short stories, *The Best of Roald Dahl*, *Roald Dahl's Book of Ghost Stories*, *The Collected Short Stories of Roald Dahl* and two volumes of autobiography, *Boy* and *Going Solo*. As a tribute to Roald Dahl on his seventieth birthday, Viking published his *Two Fables* in 1986.

Roald Dahl was one of the most successful and well-

KT-161-775

known of all children's writers. His books, which are read by children the world over, include *James and the Giant Peach*, *Charlie and the Chocolate Factory*, *The Magic Finger*, *Charlie and the Great Glass Elevator*, *Fantastic Mr Fox*, *The Twits*, *The Witches*, winner of the 1983 Whitbread Award, *The BFG* and *Matilda*.

Roald Dahl died in November 1990. *The Times* called him 'one of the most widely read and influential writers of our generation' and wrote in its obituary: 'It was well said of Dahl that he "knew how to steer an unwavering course along the hairline where the grotesque and comic meet and mingle" ... Children loved his stories and made him their favourite ... Some believe that they will be classics of the future.'

Roald Dahl

# More Tales
# of the Unexpected

Penguin Books

PENGUIN BOOKS

Published by the Penguin Group
Penguin Books Ltd, 27 Wrights Lane, London W8 5TZ, England
Penguin Books USA Inc., 375 Hudson Street, New York, New York 10014, USA
Penguin Books Australia Ltd, Ringwood, Victoria, Australia
Penguin Books Canada Ltd, 10 Alcorn Avenue, Toronto, Ontario, Canada M4V 3B2
Penguin Books (NZ) Ltd, 182–190 Wairau Road, Auckland 10, New Zealand

Penguin Books Ltd, Registered Offices: Harmondsworth, Middlesex, England

The first two stories in this book are from *Someone Like You*,
originally published by Martin Secker & Warburg Ltd in 1954
and republished by Michael Joseph Ltd in 1961. The third and fourth
stories are from *Kiss Kiss*, first published by Michael Joseph Ltd
in 1960, and the fifth is from *The Wonderful Story of Henry Sugar*,
first published by Jonathan Cape in 1977

This selection first published in Great Britain by Michael Joseph Ltd 1980
Published simultaneously in Penguin Books
20 19 18 17

Acknowledgement is hereby made to *The New Yorker* and *Playboy* in
which two of the stories included in this volume first appeared

Printed in England by Clays Ltd, St Ives plc
Set in Linotype Times

# Contents

# Contents

# Poison

It must have been around midnight when I drove home, and as I approached the gates of the bungalow I switched off the headlamps of the car so the beam wouldn't swing in through the window of the side bedroom and wake Harry Pope. But I needn't have bothered. Coming up the drive I noticed his light was still on, so he was awake anyway – unless perhaps he'd dropped off while reading.

I parked the car and went up the five steps to the balcony, counting each step carefully in the dark so I wouldn't take an extra one which wasn't there when I got to the top. I crossed the balcony, pushed through the screen doors into the house itself and switched on the light in the hall. I went across to the door of Harry's room, opened it quietly, and looked in.

He was lying on the bed and I could see he was awake. But he didn't move. He didn't even turn his head towards me, but I heard him say, 'Timber, Timber, come here.'

He spoke slowly, whispering each word carefully, separately, and I pushed the door right open and started to go quickly across the room.

'Stop. Wait a moment, Timber.' I could hardly hear what he was saying. He seemed to be straining enormously to get the words out.

'What's the matter, Harry?'

'Sshhh!' he whispered. 'Sshhh! For God's sake don't make a noise. Take your shoes off before you come nearer. *Please* do as I say, Timber.'

The way he was speaking reminded me of George Barling after he got shot in the stomach when he stood leaning against a crate containing a spare aeroplane engine, holding both hands on his stomach and saying things about the German pilot in just the same hoarse straining half whisper Harry was using now.

'Quickly, Timber, but take your shoes off first.'

I couldn't understand about taking off the shoes but I figured that if he was as ill as he sounded I'd better humour him, so I bent down and removed the shoes and left them in the middle of the floor. Then I went over to his bed.

'Don't touch the bed! For God's sake don't touch the bed!' He was still speaking like he'd been shot in the stomach and I could see him lying there on his back with a single sheet covering three-quarters of his body. He was wearing a pair of pyjamas with blue, brown, and white stripes, and he was sweating terribly. It was a hot night and I was sweating a little myself, but not like Harry. His whole face was wet and the pillow around his head was sodden with moisture. It looked like a bad go of malaria to me.

'What is it, Harry?'

'A krait,' he said.

'A *krait*! Oh, my God! Where'd it bite you? How long ago?'

'Shut up,' he whispered.

'Listen, Harry,' I said, and I leaned forward and touched his shoulder. 'We've got to be quick. Come on now, quickly, tell me where it bit you.' He was lying there very still and tense as though he was holding on to himself hard because of sharp pain.

'I haven't been bitten,' he whispered. 'Not yet. It's on my stomach. Lying there asleep.'

I took a quick pace backwards. I couldn't help it, and I stared at his stomach or rather at the sheet that covered it. The sheet was rumpled in several places and it was impossible to tell if there was anything underneath.

'You don't really mean there's a krait lying on your stomach now?'

'I swear it.'

'How did it get there?' I shouldn't have asked the question because it was easy to see he wasn't fooling. I should have told him to keep quiet.

'I was reading,' Harry said, and he spoke very slowly, taking each word in turn and speaking it carefully so as not to move the muscles of his stomach. 'Lying on my back reading and I felt something on my chest, behind the book. Sort of tickling.

8

Then out of the corner of my eye saw this little krait sliding over my pyjamas. Small, about ten inches. Knew I mustn't move. Couldn't have anyway. Lay there watching it. Thought it would go over top of the sheet.' Harry paused and was silent for a few moments. His eyes looked down along his body towards the place where the sheet covered his stomach, and I could see he was watching to make sure his whispering wasn't disturbing the thing that lay there.

'There was a fold in the sheet,' he said, speaking more slowly than ever now and so softly I had to lean close to hear him. 'See it, it's still there. It went under that. I could feel it through my pyjamas, moving on my stomach. Then it stopped moving and now it's lying there in the warmth. Probably asleep. I've been waiting for you.' He raised his eyes and looked at me.

'How long ago?'

'Hours,' he whispered. 'Hours and bloody hours and hours. I can't keep still much longer. I've been wanting to cough.'

There was not much doubt about the truth of Harry's story. As a matter of fact it wasn't a surprising thing for a krait to do. They hang around people's houses and they go for the warm places. The surprising thing was that Harry hadn't been bitten. The bite is quite deadly except sometimes when you catch it at once and they kill a fair number of people each year in Bengal, mostly in the villages.

'All right, Harry,' I said, and now I was whispering too. 'Don't move and don't talk any more unless you have to. You know it won't bite unless it's frightened. We'll fix it in no time.'

I went softly out of the room in my stocking feet and fetched a small sharp knife from the kitchen. I put it in my trouser pocket ready to use instantly in case something went wrong while we were still thinking out a plan. If Harry coughed or moved or did something to frighten the krait and got bitten, I was going to be ready to cut the bitten place and try to suck the venom out. I came back to the bedroom and Harry was still lying there very quiet and sweating all over his face. His eyes followed me as I moved across the room to his bed and I could see he was wondering what I'd been up to, I stood beside him, trying to think of the best thing to do.

'Harry,' I said, and now when I spoke I put my mouth almost

on his ear so I wouldn't have to raise my voice above the softest whisper, 'I think the best thing to do is for me to draw the sheet back very, very gently. Then we could have a look first. I think I could do that without disturbing it.'

'Don't be a damn fool.' There was no expression in his voice. He spoke each word too slowly, too carefully, and too softly for that. The expression was in the eyes and around the corners of the mouth.

'Why not?'

'The light would frighten him. It's dark under there now.'

'Then how about whipping the sheet back quick and brushing it off before it has time to strike?'

'Why don't you get a doctor?' Harry said. The way he looked at me told me I should have thought of that myself in the first place.

'A doctor. Of course. That's it. I'll get Ganderbai.'

I tiptoed out of the hall, looked up Ganderbai's number in the book, lifted the phone and told the operator to hurry.

'Dr Ganderbai,' I said. 'This is Timber Woods.'

'Hello, Mr Woods. You not in bed yet?'

'Look, could you come round at once? And bring serum – for a krait bite.'

'Who's been bitten?' The question came so sharply it was like a small explosion in my ear.

'No one. No one yet. But Harry Pope's in bed and he's got one lying on his stomach – asleep under the sheet on his stomach.'

For about three seconds there was silence on the line. Then speaking slowly, not like an explosion now but slowly, precisely, Ganderbai said, 'Tell him to keep quite still. He is not to move or to talk. Do you understand?'

'Of course.'

'I'll come at once!' He rang off and I went back to the bedroom. Harry's eyes watched me as I walked across to his bed.

'Ganderbai's coming. He said for you to lie still.'

'What in God's name does he think I'm doing!'

'Look, Harry, he said no talking. Absolutely no talking. Either of us.'

'Why don't you shut up then?' When he said this, one side of his mouth started twitching with rapid little downward movements that continued for a while after he finished speaking. I took out my handkerchief and very gently I wiped the sweat off his face and neck, and I could feel the slight twitching of the muscle – the one he used for smiling – as my fingers passed over it with the handkerchief.

I slipped out to the kitchen, got some ice from the ice-box, rolled it up in a napkin, and began to crush it small. That business of the mouth, I didn't like that. Or the way he talked, either. I carried the ice pack back to the bedroom and laid it across Harry's forehead.

'Keep you cool.'

He screwed up his eyes and drew breath sharply through his teeth. 'Take it away,' he whispered. 'Make me cough.' His smiling-muscle began to twitch again.

The beam of a headlamp shone through the window as Ganderbai's car swung around to the front of the bungalow. I went out to meet him, holding the ice pack with both hands.

'How is it?' Ganderbai asked, but he didn't stop to talk; he walked on past me across the balcony and through the screen doors into the hall. 'Where is he? Which room?'

He put his bag down on a chair in the hall and followed me into Harry's room. He was wearing soft-soled bedroom slippers and he walked across the floor noiselessly, delicately, like a careful cat. Harry watched him out of the sides of his eyes. When Ganderbai reached the bed he looked down at Harry and smiled, confident and reassuring, nodding his head to tell Harry it was a simple matter and he was not to worry but just to leave it to Dr Ganderbai. Then he turned and went back to the hall and I followed him.

'First thing is to try to get some serum into him,' he said, and he opened his bag and started to make preparations, 'Intravenously. But I must do it neatly. Don't want to make him flinch.'

We went into the kitchen and he sterilized a needle. He had a hypodermic syringe in one hand and a small bottle in the other and he stuck the needle through the rubber top of the bottle and began drawing a pale yellow liquid up into the syringe by pulling out the plunger. Then he handed the syringe to me.

'Hold that till I ask for it.'

He picked up the bag and together we returned to the room. Harry's eyes were bright now and wide open. Ganderbai bent over Harry and very cautiously, like a man handling sixteenth-century lace, he rolled up the pyjama sleeve to the elbow without moving the arm. I noticed he stood well away from the bed.

He whispered, 'I'm going to give you an injection. Serum. Just a prick but try not to move. Don't tighten your stomach muscles. Let them go limp.'

Harry looked at the syringe.

Ganderbai took a piece of red rubber tubing from his bag and slid one end under and up and around Harry's biceps; then he tied the tubing tight with a knot. He sponged a small area of the bare forearm with alcohol, handed the swab to me and took the syringe from my hand. He held it up to the light, squinting at the calibrations, squirting out some of the yellow fluid. I stood still beside him, watching. Harry was watching too and sweating all over his face so it shone like it was smeared thick with face cream melting on his skin and running down on to the pillow.

I could see the blue vein on the inside of Harry's forearm, swollen now because of the tourniquet, and then I saw the needle above the vein, Ganderbai holding the syringe almost flat against the arm, sliding the needle in sideways through the skin into the blue vein, sliding it slowly but so firmly it went in smooth as into cheese. Harry looked at the ceiling and closed his eyes and opened them again, but he didn't move.

When it was finished Ganderbai leaned forward putting his mouth close to Harry's ear. 'Now you'll be all right even if you *are* bitten. But don't move. Please don't move. I'll be back in a moment.'

He picked up his bag and went out to the hall and I followed.

'Is he safe now?' I asked.

'No.'

'How safe is he?'

The little Indian doctor stood there in the hall rubbing his lower lip.

'It must give some protection, mustn't it?' I asked.

He turned away and walked to the screen doors that led on to the verandah. I thought he was going through them, but he stopped this side of the doors and stood looking out into the night.

'Isn't the serum very good?' I asked.

'Unfortunately not,' he answered without turning round. 'It might save him. It might not. I am trying to think of something else to do.'

'Shall we draw the sheet back quick and brush it off before it has time to strike?'

'Never! We are not entitled to take a risk.' He spoke sharply and his voice was pitched a little higher than usual.

'We can't very well leave him lying there,' I said. 'He's getting nervous.'

'Please! Please!' he said, turning round, holding both hands up in the air. 'Not so fast, please. This is not a matter to rush into baldheaded.' He wiped his forehead with his handkerchief and stood there, frowning, nibbling his lip.

'You see,' he said at last. 'There is a way to do this. You know what we must do – we must administer an anaesthetic to the creature where it lies.'

It was a splendid idea.

'It is not safe,' he continued, 'because a snake is cold-blooded and anaesthetic does not work so well or so quick with such animals, but it is better than any other thing to do. We could use ether ... chloroform ...' He was speaking slowly and trying to think the thing out while he talked.

'Which shall we use?'

'Chloroform,' he said suddenly 'Ordinary chloroform. That is best. Now quick!' He took my arm and pulled me towards the balcony. 'Drive to my house! By the time you get there I will have waked up my boy on the telephone and he will show you my poisons cupboard. Here is the key of the cupboard. Take a bottle of chloroform. It has an orange label and the name is printed on it. I stay here in case anything happens. Be quick now, hurry! No, no, you don't need your shoes!'

I drove fast and in about fifteen minutes I was back with the bottle of chloroform. Ganderbai came out of Harry's room and, met me in the hall. 'You got it?' he said. 'Good, good. I just been telling him what we are going to do. But now we must hurry. It is not easy for him in there like that all this time. I am afraid he might move.'

He went back to the bedroom and I followed, carrying the bottle carefully with both hands. Harry was lying on the bed in precisely the same position as before with the sweat pouring down his cheeks. His face was white and wet. He turned his eyes towards me and I smiled at him and nodded confidently. He continued to look at me. I raised my thumb, giving him the okay signal. He closed his eyes. Ganderbai was squatting down by the bed, and on the floor beside him was the hollow rubber tube that he had previously used as a tourniquet, and he'd got a small paper funnel fitted into one end of the tube.

He began to pull a little piece of the sheet out from under the mattress. He was working directly in line with Harry's stomach, about eighteen inches from it, and I watched his fingers as they tugged gently at the edge of the sheet. He worked so slowly it was almost impossible to discern any movement either in his fingers or in the sheet that was being pulled.

Finally he succeeded in making an opening under the sheet and he took the rubber tube and inserted one end of it in the opening so that it would slide under the sheet along the mattress towards Harry's body. I do not know how long it took him to slide that tube in a few inches. It may have been twenty minutes, it may have been forty. I never once saw the tube move. I knew it was going in because the visible part of it grew gradually shorter, but I doubted that the krait could have felt even the faintest vibration. Ganderbai himself was sweating now, large pearls of sweat standing out all over his forehead and along his upper lip. But his hands were steady and I noticed that his eyes were watching, not the tube in his hands, but the area of crumpled sheet above Harry's stomach.

Without looking up, he held out a hand to me for the chloroform. I twisted out the ground-glass stopper and put the bottle right into his hand, not letting go till I was sure he had a good hold on it. Then he jerked his head for me to come closer and he whispered, 'Tell him I'm going to soak the mattress and that it will be very cold under his body. He must be ready for that and he must not move. Tell him now.'

I bent over Harry and passed on the message.

'Why doesn't he get on with it?' Harry said.

'He's going to now, Harry. But it'll feel very cold, so be ready for it.'

'Oh, God Almighty, get on, get on!' For the first time he raised his voice, and Ganderbai glanced up sharply, watched him for a few seconds, then went back to his business.

Ganderbai poured a few drops of chloroform into the paper funnel and waited while it ran down the tube. Then he poured some more. Then he waited again, and the heavy sickening smell of chloroform spread out over the room bringing with it faint unpleasant memories of white-coated nurses and white surgeons standing in a white room around a long white table. Ganderbai was pouring steadily now and I could see the heavy vapour of the chloroform swirling slowly like smoke above the paper funnel. He paused, held the bottle up to the light, poured one more funnelful and handed the bottle back to me. Slowly he drew out the rubber tube from under the sheet; then he stood up.

The strain of inserting the tube and pouring the chloroform must have been great, and I recollect that when Ganderbai turned and whispered to me, his voice was small and tired, 'We'll give it fifteen minutes. Just to be safe.'

I leaned over to tell Harry. 'We're going to give it fifteen minutes, just to be safe. But it's probably done for already.'

'Then why for God's sake don't you look and see!' Again he spoke loudly and Ganderbai sprang round, his small brown face suddenly very angry. He had almost pure black eyes and he stared at Harry and Harry's smiling-muscle started to twitch. I took my handkerchief and wiped his wet face, trying to stroke his forehead a little for comfort as I did so.

Then we stood and waited beside the bed, Ganderbai watching Harry's face all the time in a curious intense manner. The little Indian was concentrating all his will power on keeping

Harry quiet. He never once took his eyes from the patient and although he made no sound, he seemed somehow to be shouting at him all the time, saying: Now listen, you've got to listen, you're not going to go spoiling this now, d'you hear me; and Harry lay there twitching his mouth, sweating, closing his eyes, opening them, looking at me, at the sheet, at the ceiling, at me again, but never at Ganderbai. Yet somehow Ganderbai was holding him. The smell of chloroform was oppressive and it made me feel sick, but I couldn't leave the room now. I had the feeling someone was blowing up a huge balloon and I could see it was going to burst, but I couldn't look away.

At length Ganderbai turned and nodded and I knew he was ready to proceed. 'You go over to the other side of the bed,' he said. 'We will each take one side of the sheet and draw it back together, but very slowly, please, and very quietly.'

'Keep still now, Harry,' I said and I went around to the other side of the bed and took hold of the sheet. Ganderbai stood opposite me, and together we began to draw back the sheet, lifting it up clear of Harry's body, taking it back very slowly, both of us standing well away but at the same time bending forward, trying to peer underneath it. The smell of chloroform was awful. I remember trying to hold my breath and when I couldn't do that any longer I tried to breathe shallow so the stuff wouldn't get into my lungs.

The whole of Harry's chest was visible now, or rather the striped pyjama top which covered it, and then I saw the white cord of his pyjama trousers, neatly tied in a bow. A little farther and I saw a button, a mother-of-pearl button, and that was something I had never had on my pyjamas, a fly button, let alone a mother-of-pearl one. This Harry, I thought, he is very refined. It is odd how one sometimes has frivolous thoughts at exciting moments, and I distinctly remember thinking about Harry being very refined when I saw that button.

Apart from the button there was nothing on his stomach.

We pulled the sheet back faster then, and when we had uncovered his legs and feet we let the sheet drop over the end of the bed on to the floor.

'Don't move,' Ganderbai said, 'don't move, Mr Pope', and he began to peer around along the side of Harry's body and under his legs.

'We must be careful,' he said. 'It may be anywhere. It could be up the leg of his pyjamas.'

When Ganderbai said this, Harry quickly raised his head from the pillow and looked down at his legs. It was the first time he had moved. Then suddenly he jumped up, stood on his bed and shook his legs one after the other violently in the air. At that moment we both thought he had been bitten and Ganderbai was already reaching down into his bag for a scalpel and a tourniquet when Harry ceased his caperings and stood still and looked at the mattress he was standing on and shouted, 'It's not there!'

Ganderbai straightened up and for a moment he too looked at the mattress; then he looked up at Harry. Harry was all right. He hadn't been bitten and now he wasn't going to get bitten and he wasn't going to be killed and everything was fine. But that didn't seem to make anyone feel any better.

'Mr Pope, you are of course *quite* sure you saw it in the first place?' There was a note of sarcasm in Ganderbai's voice that he would never have employed in ordinary circumstances. 'You don't think you might possibly have been dreaming, do you, Mr Pope?' The way Ganderbai was looking at Harry, I realized that the sarcasm was not seriously intended. He was only easing up a bit after the strain.

Harry stood on his bed in his striped pyjamas, glaring at Ganderbai, and the colour began to spread out over his cheeks.

'Are you telling me I'm a liar?' he shouted.

Ganderbai remained absolutely still, watching Harry. Harry took a pace forward on the bed and there was a shining look in his eyes.

'Why, you dirty little Hindu sewer rat!'

'Shut up, Harry!' I said.

'You dirty black –'

'Harry!' I called. 'Shut up, Harry!' It was terrible, the things he was saying.

Ganderbai went out of the room as though neither of us was

there and I followed him and put my arm around his shoulder as he walked across the hall and out on to the balcony.

'Don't you listen to Harry,' I said. 'This thing's made him so he doesn't know what he's saying.'

We went down the steps from the balcony to the drive and across the drive in the darkness to where his old Morris car was parked. He opened the door and got in.

'You did a wonderful job,' I said. 'Thank you so very much for coming.'

'All he needs is a good holiday,' he said quietly, without looking at me, then he started the engine and drove off.

# The Sound Machine

It was a warm summer evening and Klausner walked quickly through the front gate and around the side of the house and into the garden at the back. He went on down the garden until he came to a wooden shed and he unlocked the door, went inside and closed the door behind him.

The interior of the shed was an unpainted room. Against one wall, on the left, there was a long wooden workbench, and on it, among a littering of wires and batteries and small sharp tools, there stood a black box about three feet long, the shape of a child's coffin.

Klausner moved across the room to the box. The top of the box was open, and he bent down and began to poke and peer inside it among a mass of different-coloured wires and silver tubes. He picked up a piece of paper that lay beside the box, studied it carefully, put it down, peered inside the box and started running his fingers along the wires, tugging gently at them to test the connections, glancing back at the paper, then into the box, then at the paper again, checking each wire. He did this for perhaps an hour.

Then he put a hand around to the front of the box where there were three dials, and he began to twiddle them, watching at the same time the movement of the mechanism inside the box. All the while he kept speaking softly to himself, nodding his head, smiling sometimes, his hands always moving, the fingers moving swiftly, deftly, inside the box, his mouth twisting into curious shapes when a thing was delicate or difficult to do, saying, 'Yes ... Yes ... And now this one ... Yes ... Yes. But is this right? Is it – where's my diagram? ... Ah, yes ... Of course ... Yes, yes ... That's right ... And now ... Good ... Good ... Yes ... Yes, yes, yes.' His concentration was intense; his movements were quick; there was an air of urgency about

19

the way he worked, of breathlessness, of strong suppressed excitement.

Suddenly he heard footsteps on the gravel path outside and he straightened and turned swiftly as the door opened and a tall man came in. It was Scott. It was only Scott, the doctor.

'Well, well, well,' the Doctor said. 'So this is where you hide yourself in the evenings.'

'Hullo, Scott,' Klausner said.

'I happened to be passing,' the Doctor told him, 'so I dropped in to see how you were. There was no one in the house, so I came on down here. How's that throat of yours been behaving?'

'It's all right. It's fine.'

'Now I'm here I might as well have a look at it.'

'Please don't trouble. I'm quite cured. I'm fine.'

The Doctor began to feel the tension in the room. He looked at the black box on the bench, then he looked at the man. 'You've got your hat on,' he said.

'Oh, have I?' Klausner reached up, removed the hat, and put it on the bench.

The Doctor came up closer and bent down to look into the box. 'What's this?' he said. 'Making a radio?'

'No, just fooling around.'

'It's got rather complicated-looking innards.'

'Yes,' Klausner seemed tense and distracted.

'What is it?' the Doctor asked. 'It's rather a frightening-looking thing, isn't it?'

'It's just an idea.'

'Yes?'

'It has to do with sound, that's all.'

'Good heavens, man! Don't you get enough of that sort of thing all day in your work?'

'I like sound.'

'So it seems.' The Doctor went to the door, turned, and said, 'Well, I won't disturb you. Glad your throat's not worrying you any more.' But he kept standing there looking at the box, intrigued by the remarkable complexity of its inside, curious to know what this strange patient of his was up to. 'What's it really for?' he asked. 'You've made me inquisitive.'

Klausner looked down at the box, then at the Doctor, and he reached up and began gently to scratch the lobe of his right ear. There was a pause. The Doctor stood by the door, waiting, smiling.

'All right, I'll tell you, if you're interested.' There was another pause, and the Doctor could see that Klausner was having trouble about how to begin.

He was shifting from one foot to the other, tugging at the lobe of his ear, looking at his feet, and then at last, slowly, he said, 'Well, it's like this ... the theory is very simple really. The human ear ... you know that it can't hear everything. There are sounds that are so low-pitched or so high-pitched that it can't hear them.'

'Yes,' the Doctor said. 'Yes.'

'Well, speaking very roughly, any note so high that it has more than fifteen thousand vibrations a second – we can't hear it. Dogs have better ears than us. You know you can buy a whistle whose note is so high-pitched that you can't hear it at all. But a dog can hear it.'

'Yes, I've seen one,' the Doctor said.

'Of course you have. And up the scale, higher than the note of that whistle, there is another note – a vibration if you like, but I prefer to think of it as a note. You can't hear that one either. And above that there is another and another rising right up the scale for ever and ever and ever, an endless succession of notes ... an infinity of notes ... there is a note – if only our ears could hear it – so high that it vibrates a million times a second ... and another a million times as high as that ... and on and on, higher and higher, as far as numbers go, which is ... infinity ... eternity ... beyond the stars.'

Klausner was becoming more animated every moment. He was a small frail man, nervous and twitchy, with always moving hands. His large head inclined towards his left shoulder as though his neck were not quite strong enough to support it rigidly. His face was smooth and pale, almost white, and the pale-grey eyes that blinked and peered from behind a pair of steel spectacles were bewildered, unfocused, remote. He was a frail, nervous, twitchy little man, a moth of a man, dreamy and distracted; suddenly fluttering and animated; and now the

Doctor, looking at that strange pale face and those pale-grey eyes, felt that somehow there was about this little person a quality of distance, of immense immeasurable distance, as though the mind were far away from where the body was.

The Doctor waited for him to go on. Klausner sighed and clasped his hands tightly together. 'I believe,' he said, speaking more slowly now, 'that there is a whole world of sound about us all the time that we cannot hear. It is possible that up there in those high-pitched inaudible regions there is a new exciting music being made, with subtle harmonies and fierce grinding discords, a music so powerful that it would drive us mad if only our ears were tuned to hear the sound of it. There may be anything ... for all we know there may –'

'Yes,' the Doctor said. 'But it's not very probable.'

'Why not? Why not?' Klausner pointed to a fly sitting on a small roll of copper wire on the workbench. 'You see that fly? What sort of a noise is that fly making now? None – that one can hear. But for all we know the creature may be whistling like mad on a very high note, or barking or croaking or singing a song. It's got a mouth, hasn't it? It's got a throat!'

The Doctor looked at the fly and he smiled. He was still standing by the door with his hands on the doorknob. 'Well,' he said. 'So you're going to check up on that?'

'Some time ago,' Klausner said, 'I made a simple instrument that proved to me the existence of many odd inaudible sounds. Often I have sat and watched the needle of my instrument recording the presence of sound vibrations in the air when I myself could hear nothing. And *those* are the sounds I want to listen to. I want to know where they come from and who or what is making them.'

'And that machine on the table there,' the Doctor said, 'is that going to allow you to hear these noises?'

'It may. Who knows? So far, I've had no luck. But I've made some changes in it and tonight I'm ready for another trial. This machine,' he said, touching it with his hands, 'is designed to pick up sound vibrations that are too high-pitched for reception by the human ear, and to convert them to a scale of audible tones. I tune it in, almost like a radio.'

'How d'you mean?'

'It isn't complicated. Say I wish to listen to the squeak of a bat. That's a fairly high-pitched sound – about thirty thousand vibrations a second. The average human ear can't quite hear it. Now, if there were a bat flying around this room and I tuned in to thirty thousand on my machine, I would hear the squeaking of that bat very clear. I would even hear the correct note – F sharp, or B flat, or whatever it might be – but merely at a much *lower pitch*. Don't you understand?'

The Doctor looked at the long, black coffin-box. 'And you're going to try it tonight?'

'Yes.'

'Well, I wish you luck.' He glanced at his watch. 'My goodness!' he said. 'I must fly. Good-bye, and thank you for telling me. I must call again some time and find out what happened.' The Doctor went out and closed the door behind him.

For a while longer, Klausner fussed about with the wires in the black box; then he straightened up and in a soft excited whisper said, 'Now we'll try again . . . We'll take it out into the garden this time . . . and then perhaps . . . perhaps . . . the reception will be better. Lift it up now . . . carefully . . . Oh, my God, it's heavy!' He carried the box to the door, found that he couldn't open the door without putting it down, carried it back, put it on the bench, opened the door, and then carried it with some difficulty into the garden. He placed the box carefully on a small wooden table that stood on the lawn. He returned to the shed and fetched a pair of earphones. He plugged the wire connections from the earphones into the machine and put the earphones over his ears. The movements of his hands were quick and precise. He was excited, and breathed loudly and quickly through his mouth. He kept on talking to himself with little words of comfort and encouragement, as though he were afraid – afraid that the machine might not work and afraid also of what might happen if it did.

He stood there in the garden beside the wooden table, so pale, small, and thin that he looked like an ancient, consumptive, bespectacled child. The sun had gone down. There was no wind, no sound at all. From where he stood, he could see over a low fence into the next garden, and there was a woman walking down the garden with a flower-basket on her arm. He watched her for a while without thinking about her at all. Then he turned to the box on the table and pressed a switch on its front. He put his left hand on the volume control and his right hand on the knob that moved a needle across a large central dial, like the wavelength dial of a radio. The dial was marked with many numbers, in a series of bands, startng at 15,000 and going on up to 1,000,000.

And now he was bending forward over the machine. His head was cocked to one side in a tense, listening attitude. His right hand was beginning to turn the knob. The needle was travelling slowly across the dial, so slowly he could hardly see it move, and in the earphones he could hear a faint, spasmodic crackling.

Behind this crackling sound he could hear a distant humming tone which was the noise of the machine itself, but that was all. As he listened, he became conscious of a curious sensation, a feeling that his ears were stretching out away from his head, that each ear was connected to his head by a thin stiff wire, like a tentacle, and that the wires were lengthening, that the ears were going up and up towards a secret and forbidden territory, a dangerous ultrasonic region where ears had never been before and had no right to be.

The little needle crept slowly across the dial, and suddenly he heard a shriek, a frightful piercing shriek, and he jumped and dropped his hands, catching hold of the edge of the table. He stared around him as if expecting to see the person who had shrieked. There was no one in sight except the woman in the garden next door, and it was certainly not she. She was bending down, cutting yellow roses and putting them in her basket.

Again it came – a throatless, inhuman shriek, sharp and short, very clear and cold. The note itself possessed a minor, metallic quality that he had never heard before. Klausner looked around him, searching instinctively for the source of the noise. The woman next door was the only living thing in sight. He saw her reach down, take a rose stem in the fingers of one hand and snip the stem with a pair of scissors. Again he heard the scream.

It came at the exact moment when the rose stem was cut.

At this point, the woman straightened up, put the scissors in the basket with the roses, and turned to walk away.

'Mrs Saunders!' Klausner shouted, his voice shrill with excitement. 'Oh, Mrs Saunders!'

And looking round, the woman saw her neighbour standing on his lawn – a fantastic, arm-waving little person with a pair of earphones on his head – calling to her in a voice so high and loud that she became alarmed.

'Cut another one! Please cut another one quickly!'

She stood still, staring at him. 'Why, Mr Klausner,' she said. 'What's the matter?'

'Please do as I ask,' he said. 'Cut just one more rose!'

Mrs Saunders had always believed her neighbour to be a rather peculiar person; now it seemed that he had gone completely crazy. She wondered whether she should run into the house and fetch her husband. No, she thought. No, he's harmless. I'll just humour him. 'Certainly, Mr Klausner, if you like,' she said. She took her scissors from the basket, bent down, and snipped another rose.

Again Klausner heard that frightful, throatless shriek in the earphones; again it came at the exact moment the rose stem was cut. He took off the earphones and ran to the fence that separated the two gardens. 'All right,' he said. 'That's enough. No more. Please, no more.'

The woman stood there, a yellow rose in one hand, clippers in the other, looking at him.

'I'm going to tell you something, Mrs Saunders,' he said, 'something that you won't believe.' He put his hands on top of the fence and peered at her intently through his thick spectacles. 'You have, this evening, cut a basketful of roses. You have with a sharp pair of scissors cut through the stems of living things, and each rose that you cut screamed in the most terrible way. Did you know that, Mrs Saunders?'

'No,' she said. 'I certainly didn't know that.'

'It happens to be true,' he said. He was breathing rather

rapidly, but he was trying to control his excitement. 'I heard them shrieking. Each time you cut one, I heard the cry of pain. A very high-pitched sound, approximately one hundred and thirty-two thousand vibrations a second. You couldn't possibly have heard it yourself. But *I* heard it.'

'Did you really, Mr Klausner?' She decided she would make a dash for the house in about five seconds.

'You might say,' he went on, 'that a rose bush has no nervous system to feel with, no throat to cry with. You'd be right. It hasn't. Not like ours, anyway. But *how do you know, Mrs Saunders*' - and here he leaned far over the fence and spoke in a fierce whisper - '*how do you know* that a rose bush doesn't feel as much pain when someone cuts its stem in two as you would feel if someone cut your wrist off with a garden shears? *How do you know that?* It's *alive*, isn't it?'

'Yes, Mr Klausner. Oh, yes - and good night.' Quickly she turned and ran up the garden to her house. Klausner went back to the table. He put on the earphones and stood for a while listening. He could still hear the faint crackling sound and the humming noise of the machine, but nothing more. He bent down and took hold of a small white daisy growing on the lawn. He took it between thumb and forefinger and slowly pulled it upward and sideways until the stem broke.

From the moment that he started pulling to the moment when the stem broke, he heard - he distinctly heard in the earphones - a faint high-pitched cry, curiously inanimate. He took another daisy and did it again. Once more he heard the cry, but he wasn't so sure now that it expressed *pain*. No, it wasn't pain; it was surprise. Or was it? It didn't really express any of the feelings or emotions known to a human being. It was just a cry, a neutral, stony cry - a single emotionless note, expressing nothing. It had been the same with the roses. He had been wrong in calling it a cry of pain. A flower probably didn't feel pain. It felt something else which we didn't know about - something called toin or spurl or plinuckment, or anything you like.

He stood up and removed the earphones. It was getting dark and he could see pricks of light shining in the windows of the houses all around him. Carefully he picked up the black box from the table, carried it into the shed and put it on the work-bench. Then he went out, locked the door behind him, and walked up to the house.

The next morning Klausner was up as soon as it was light. He dressed and went straight to the shed. He picked up the machine and carried it outside, clasping it to his chest with both hands, walking unsteadily under its weight. He went past the house, out through the front gate, and across the road to the park. There he paused and looked around him; then he went on until he came to a large tree, a beech tree, and he placed the machine on the ground close to the trunk of the tree. Quickly he went back to the house and got an axe from the coal cellar and carried it across the road into the park. He put the axe on the ground beside the tree.

Then he looked around him again, peering nervously through his thick glasses in every direction. There was no one about. It was six in the morning.

He put the earphones on his head and switched on the machine. He listened for a moment to the faint familiar hum-ming sound; then he picked up the axe, took a stance with his legs wide apart, and swung the axe as hard as he could at the base of the tree trunk. The blade cut deep into the wood and stuck there, and at the instant of impact he heard a most ex-traordinary noise in the earphones. It was a new noise, unlike any he had heard before – a harsh, noteless, enormous noise, a growling, low-pitched, screaming sound, not quick and short like the noise of the roses, but drawn out like a sob lasting for fully a minute, loudest at the moment when the axe struck, fading gradually fainter and fainter until it was gone.

Klausner stared in horror at the place where the blade of the axe had sunk into the woodflesh of the tree; then gently he took the axe handle, worked the blade loose and threw the thing to the ground. With his fingers he touched the gash that the axe had made in the wood, touching the edges of the gash, trying to press them together to close the wound, and he kept saying, 'Tree . . . oh, tree . . . I am sorry . . . I am so sorry . . . but it will heal . . . it will heal fine . . .'

For a while he stood there with his hands upon the trunk of the great tree; then suddenly he turned away and hurried off out of the park, across the road, through the front gate and back into his house. He went to the telephone, consulted the book, dialled a number and waited. He held the receiver tightly in his left hand and tapped the table impatiently with his right. He heard the telephone buzzing at the other end, and then the click of a lifted receiver and a man's voice, a sleepy voice, saying: 'Hullo. Yes.'

'Dr Scott?' he said.

'Yes. Speaking.'

'Dr Scott. You must come at once – quickly, please.'

'Who is it speaking?'

'Klausner here, and you remember what I told you last night about my experience with sound, and how I hoped I might –'

'Yes, yes, of course, but what's the matter? Are you ill?'

'No, I'm not ill, but –'

'It's half-past six in the morning,' the Doctor sad, 'and you call me but you are not ill.'

'Please come. Come quickly. I want someone to hear it. It's driving me mad! I can't believe it ...'

The Doctor heard the frantic, almost hysterical note in the man's voice, the same note he was used to hearing in the voices of people who called up and said, 'There's been an accident. Come quickly.' He said slowly, 'You really want me to get out of bed and come over now?'

'Yes, now. At once, please.'

'All right, then – I'll come.'

Klausner sat down beside the telephone and waited. He tried to remember what the shriek of the tree had sounded like, but he couldn't. He could remember only that it had been enormous and frightful and that it had made him feel sick with horror. He tried to imagine what sort of noise a human would make if he had to stand anchored to the ground while someone deliberately swung a small sharp thing at his leg so that the blade cut in deep and wedged itself in the cut. Same sort of noise perhaps? No. Quite different. The noise of the tree was worse than any known human noise because of that frightening, toneless, throatless quality. He began to wonder about other living things, and he thought immediately of a field of wheat, a field of wheat standing up straight and yellow and alive, with the mower going through it, cutting the stems, five hundred stems a second, every second. Oh, my God, what would *that* noise be like? Five hundred wheat plants screaming together and every second another five hundred being cut and screaming and – no, he thought, I do not want to go to a wheat field with my machine. I would never eat bread after that. But what about potatoes and cabbages and carrots and onions? And what about apples? Ah, no. Apples are all right. They fall off naturally when they are ripe. Apples are all right if you let them fall off instead of tearing them from the tree branch. But not vegetables. Not a potato for example. A potato would surely shriek; so would a carrot and an onion and a cabbage ...

He heard the click of the front-gate latch and he jumped up and went out and saw the tall doctor coming down the path, little black bag in hand.

'Well,' the Doctor said. 'Well, what's all the trouble?'

'Come with me, Doctor. I want you to hear it. I called you because you're the only one I've told. It's over the road in the park. Will you come now?'

The Doctor looked at him. He seemed calmer now. There was no sign of madness or hysteria, he was merely disturbed and excited.

They went across the road into the park and Klausner led the way to the great beech tree at the foot of which stood the long black coffin-box of the machine – and the axe.

'Why did you bring it out here?' the Doctor asked.

'I wanted a tree. There aren't any big trees in the garden.'

'And why the axe?'

'You'll see in a moment. But now please put on these earphones and listen. Listen carefully and tell me afterwards precisely what you hear. I want to make quite sure ...'

The Doctor smiled and took the earphones and put them over his ears.

Klausner bent down and flicked the switch on the panel of the machine, then he picked up the axe and took his stance with his legs apart, ready to swing. For a moment he paused.

'Can you hear anything?' he said to the Doctor.

'Can I what?'

'Can you *hear* anything?'

'Just a humming noise.'

Klausner stood there with the axe in his hands trying to bring himself to swing, but the thought of the noise that the tree would make made him pause again.

'What are you waiting for?' the Doctor asked.

'Nothing,' Klausner answered, and then he lifted the axe and swung it at the tree, and as he swung, he thought he felt, he could swear he felt a movement of the ground on which he stood. He felt a slight shifting of the earth beneath his feet as though the roots of the tree were moving underneath the soil, but it was too late to check the blow and the axe blade struck the tree and wedged deep into the wood. At that moment, high overhead, there was the cracking sound of wood splintering and the swishing sound of leaves brushing against other leaves and they both looked up and the Doctor cried, 'Watch out! Run, man! Quickly, run!'

The Doctor had ripped off the earphones and was running away fast, but Klausner stood spellbound, staring up at the great branch, sixty feet long at least, that was bending slowly downward, breaking and crackling and splintering at its thickest point, where it joined the main trunk of the tree. The branch came crashing down and Klausner leapt aside just in time. It fell upon the machine and smashed it into pieces.

'Great heavens!' shouted the Doctor as he came running back. 'That was a near one! I thought it had got you!'

Klausner was staring at the tree. His large head was leaning to one side and upon his smooth white face there was a tense, horrified expression. Slowly he walked up to the tree and gently he prised the blade loose from the trunk.

'Did you hear it?' he said, turning to the Doctor. His voice was barely audible.

The Doctor was still out of breath from running and the excitement. 'Hear what?'

'In the earphones. Did you hear anything when the axe struck?'

The Doctor began to rub the back of his neck. 'Well,' he said, 'as a matter of fact ...' He paused and frowned and bit his lower lip. 'No, I'm not sure. I couldn't be sure. I don't suppose I had the earphones on for more than a second after the axe struck.'

'Yes, yes, but what did you hear?'

'I don't know,' the Doctor said. 'I don't know what I heard. Probably the noise of the branch breaking.' He was speaking rapidly, rather irritably.

'What did it sound like?' Klausner leaned forward slightly, staring hard at the Doctor. '*Exactly* what did it sound like?'

'Oh, hell!' the Doctor said. 'I really don't know. I was more interested in getting out of the way. Let's leave it.'

'Dr Scott, *what-did-it-sound-like*?'

'For God's sake, how could I tell, what with half the tree falling on me and having to run for my life?' The Doctor certainly seemed nervous. Klausner had sensed it now. He stood quite still, staring at the Doctor and for fully half a minute he didn't speak. The Doctor moved his feet, shrugged his shoulders and half turned to go. 'Well,' he said, 'we'd better get back.'

'Look,' said the little man, and now his smooth white face became suddenly suffused with colour. 'Look,' he said, 'you stitch this up.' He pointed to the last gash that the axe had made in the tree trunk. 'You stitch this up quickly.'

'Don't be silly,' the Doctor said.

'You do as I say. Stitch it up.' Klausner was gripping the axe handle and he spoke softly, in a curious, almost a threatening tone.

'Don't be silly,' the Doctor said. 'I can't stitch through wood. Come on. Let's get back.'

'So you can't stitch through wood?'

'No, of course not.'

'Have you got any iodine in your bag?'

'What if I have?'

'Then paint the cut with iodine. It'll sting, but that can't be helped.'

'Now look,' the Doctor said, and again he turned as if to go. 'Let's not be ridiculous. Let's get back to the house and then ...'

'*Paint-the-cut-with-iodine.*'

The Doctor hesitated. He saw Klausner's hands tightening

31

on the handle of the axe. He decided that his only alternative was to run away fast, and he certainly wasn't going to do that.

'All right,' he said. 'I'll paint it with iodine.'

He got his black bag which was lying on the grass about ten yards away, opened it and took out a bottle of iodine and some cotton wool. He went up to the tree trunk, uncorked the bottle, tipped some of the iodine on to the cotton wool, bent down, and began to dab it into the cut. He kept one eye on Klausner who was standing motionless with the axe in his hands, watching him.

'Make sure you get it right in.'

'Yes,' the Doctor said.

'Now do the other one – the one just above it!'

The Doctor did as he was told.

'There you are,' he said. 'It's done.'

He straightened up and surveyed his work in a very serious manner. 'That should do nicely.'

Klausner came closer and gravely examined the two wounds.

'Yes,' he said, nodding his huge head slowly up and down. 'Yes, that will do nicely.' He stepped back a pace. 'You'll come and look at them again tomorrow?'

'Oh, yes,' the Doctor said. 'Of course.'

'And put some more iodine on?'

'If necessary, yes.'

'Thank you, Doctor,' Klausner said, and he nodded his head again and he dropped the axe and all at once he smiled, a wild, excited smile, and quickly the Doctor went over to him and gently he took him by the arm and he said, 'Come on, we must go now,' and suddenly they were walking away, the two of them, walking silently, rather hurriedly across the park, over the road, back to the house.

# Georgy Porgy

Without in any way wishing to blow my own trumpet, I think that I can claim to being in most respects a moderately well-matured and rounded individual. I have travelled a good deal. I am adequately read. I speak Greek and Latin. I dabble in science. I can tolerate a mildly liberal attitude in the politics of others. I have compiled a volume of notes upon the evolution of the madrigal in the fifteenth century. I have witnessed the death of a large number of persons in their beds, and in addition, I have influenced, at least I hope I have, the lives of quite a few others by the spoken word delivered from the pulpit.

Yet in spite of all this, I must confess that I have never in my life – well, how shall I put it? – I have never really had anything much to do with women.

To be perfectly honest, up until three weeks ago I had never so much as laid a finger on one of them except perhaps to help her over a stile or something like that when the occasion demanded. And even then I always tried to ensure that I touched only the shoulder or the waist or some other place where the skin was covered, because the one thing I never could stand was actual contact between my skin and theirs. Skin touching skin, my skin, that is, touching the skin of a female, whether it were leg, neck, face, hand, or merely finger, was so repugnant to me that I invariably greeted a lady with my hands clasped firmly behind my back to avoid the inevitable handshake.

I could go further than that and say that any sort of physical contact with them, even when the skin wasn't bare, would disturb me considerably. If a woman stood close to me in a queue so that our bodies touched, or if she squeezed in beside me on a bus seat, hip to hip and thigh to thigh, my cheeks would begin burning like mad and little prickles of sweat would start coming out all over the crown of my head.

This condition is all very well in a schoolboy who has just reached the age of puberty. With him it is simply Dame Nature's way of putting on the brakes and holding the lad back until he is old enough to behave like a gentleman. I approve of that.

But there was no reason on God's earth why I, at the ripe old age of thirty-one, should continue to suffer a similar embarrassment. I was well trained to resist temptation, and I was certainly not given to vulgar passions.

Had I been even the slightest bit ashamed of my own personal appearance, then that might possibly have explained the whole thing. But I was not. On the contrary, and though I say it myself, the fates had been rather kind to me in that regard. I stood exactly five and a half feet tall in my stockinged feet, and my shoulders, though they sloped downward a little from the neck, were nicely in balance with my small neat frame. (Personally, I've always thought that a little slope on the shoulder lends a subtle and faintly aesthetic air to a man who is not overly tall, don't you agree?) My features were regular, my teeth were in excellent condition (protruding only a smallish amount from the upper jaw), and my hair, which was an unusually brilliant ginger-red, grew thickly all over my scalp. Good heavens above, I had seen men who were perfect shrimps in comparison with me displaying an astonishing aplomb in their dealings with the fairer sex. And oh, how I envied them! How I longed to do likewise - to be able to share in a few of those pleasant little rituals of contact that I observed continually taking place between men and women - the touching of hands, the peck on the cheek, the linking of arms, the pressure of knee against knee or foot against foot under the dining-table, and most of all, the full-blown violent embrace that comes when two of them join together on the floor - for a dance.

But such things were not for me. Alas, I had to spend my time avoiding them instead. And this, my friends, was easier said than done, even for a humble curate in a small country region far from the fleshpots of the metropolis.

My flock, you understand, contained an inordinate number of ladies. There were scores of them in the parish, and the unfortunate thing about it was that at least sixty per cent of them were spinsters, completely untamed by the benevolent influence of holy matrimony.

I tell you I was jumpy as a squirrel.

One would have thought that with all the careful training my mother had given me as a child, I should have been capable of taking this sort of thing well in my stride, and no doubt I would have done if only she had lived long enough to complete my education. But alas, she was killed when I was still quite young.

She was a wonderful woman, my mother. She used to wear huge bracelets on her wrists, five or six of them at a time, with all sorts of things hanging from them and tinkling against each other as she moved. It didn't matter where she was, you could always find her by listening for the noise of those bracelets. It was better than a cowbell. And in the evenings she used to sit on the sofa in her black trousers with her feet tucked up underneath her, smoking endless cigarettes from a long black holder. And I'd be crouching on the floor, watching her.

'You want to taste my martini, George?' she used to ask.

'Now stop it, Clare,' my father would say. 'If you're not careful you'll stunt the boy's growth.'

'Go on,' she said. 'Don't be frightened of it. Drink it.'

I always did everything my mother told me.

'That's enough,' my father said. 'He only has to know what it tastes like.'

'Please don't interfere, Boris. This is *very* important.'

My mother had a theory that nothing in the world should be kept secret from a child. Show him everything. Make him *experience* it.

'I'm not going to have any boy of mine going around whispering dirty secrets with other children and having to guess about this thing and that simply because no one will tell him.'

Tell him everything. Make him listen.

'Come over here, George, and I'll tell you what there is to know about God.'

She never read stories to me at night before I went to bed; she just 'told' me things instead. And every evening it was something different.

'Come over here, George, because now I'm going to tell you about Mohammed.'

She would be sitting on the sofa in her black trousers with her legs crossed and her feet tucked up underneath her, and she'd beckon to me in a queer languorous manner with the hand that held the long black cigarette-holder, and the bangles would start jingling all the way up her arm.

'If you must have a religion I suppose Mohammedanism is as good as any of them. It's all based on keeping healthy. You have lots of wives, and you mustn't ever smoke or drink.'

'Why mustn't you smoke or drink, Mummy?'

'Because if you've got lots of wives you have to keep healthy and virile.'

'What is virile?'

'I'll go into that tomorrow, my pet. Let's deal with one subject at a time. Another thing about the Mohammedan is that he never never gets constipated.'

'Now, Clare,' my father would say, looking up from his book. 'Stick to the facts.'

'My dear Boris, you don't know anything about it. Now if only *you* would try bending forward and touching the ground with your forehead morning, noon, and night every day, facing Mecca, you might have a bit less trouble in that direction yourself.'

I used to love listening to her, even though I could only understand about half of what she was saying. She really was telling me secrets, and there wasn't anything more exciting than that.

'Come over here, George, and I'll tell you precisely how your father makes his money.'

'Now, Clare, that's quite enough.'

'Nonsense, darling. Why make a *secret* out of it with the child? He'll only imagine something much much worse.'

I was exactly ten years old when she started giving me detailed lectures on the subject of sex. This was the biggest secret of them all, and therefore the most enthralling.

'Come over here, George, because now I'm going to tell you how you came into this world, right from the very beginning.'

I saw my father glance up quietly, and open his mouth wide the way he did when he was going to say something vital, but my mother was already fixing him with those brilliant shining eyes of hers, and he went slowly back to his book without uttering a sound.

'Your poor father is embarrassed,' she said, and she gave me her private smile, the one that she gave nobody else, only to me – the one-sided smile where just one corner of her mouth lifted slowly upward until it made a lovely long wrinkle that stretched right up to the eye itself, and became a sort of wink-smile instead.

'Embarrassment, my pet, is the one thing that I want you never to feel. And don't think for a moment that your father is embarrassed only because of *you*.'

My father started wriggling about in his chair.

'My God, he's even embarrassed about things like that when he's alone with me, his own wife.'

'About things like what?' I asked.

At that point my father got up and quietly left the room.

I think it must have been about a week after this that my mother was killed. It may possibly have been a little later, ten days or a fortnight, I can't be sure. All I know is that we were getting near the end of this particular series of 'talks' when it happened; and because I myself was personally involved in the brief chain of events that led up to her death, I can still remember every single detail of that curious night just as clearly as if it were yesterday. I can switch it on in my memory any time I like and run it through in front of my eyes exactly as though it were the reel of a cinema film; and it never varies. It always ends at precisely the same place, no more and no less, and it always begins in the same peculiarly sudden way, with the screen in darkness, and my mother's voice somewhere above me, calling my name:

'George! Wake up, George, wake up!'

And then there is a bright electric light dazzling in my eyes, and right from the very centre of it, but far away, the voice is still calling me:

'George, wake up and get out of bed and put your dressing-gown on! Quickly! You're coming downstairs. There's something I want you to see. Come on, child, come on! Hurry up! And put your slippers on. We're going outside.'

'Outside?'

'Don't argue with me, George. Just do as you're told.' I am so sleepy I can hardly see to walk, but my mother takes me firmly by the hand and leads me downstairs and out through the front door into the night where the cold air is like a sponge of water in my face, and I open my eyes wide and see the lawn all sparkling with frost and the cedar tree with its tremendous arms standing black against a thin small moon. And overhead a great mass of stars is wheeling up into the sky.

We hurry across the lawn, my mother and I, her bracelets all jingling like mad and me having to trot to keep up with her. Each step I take I can feel the crisp frosty grass crunching softly underfoot.

'Josephine has just started having her babies,' my mother says. 'It's a perfect opportunity. You shall watch the whole process.'

There is a light burning in the garage when we get there, and we go inside. My father isn't there, nor is the car, and the place seems huge and bare, and the concrete floor is freezing cold through the soles of my bedroom slippers. Josephine is reclining on a heap of straw inside the low wire cage in one corner of the room – a large blue rabbit with small pink eyes that watch us suspiciously as we go towards her. The husband, whose name is Napoleon, is now in a separate cage in the opposite corner, and I notice that he is standing on his hind legs scratching impatiently at the netting.

'Look!' my mother cries. 'She's just having the first one! It's almost out!'

We both creep closer to Josephine, and I squat down beside the cage with my face right up against the wire. I am fascinated. Here is one rabbit coming out of another. It is magical and rather splendid. It is also very quick.

'Look how it comes out all neatly wrapped up in its own little cellophane bag!' my mother is saying.

'And just look how she's taking care of it now! The poor darling doesn't have a face-flannel, and even if she did she couldn't hold it in her paws, so she's washing it with her tongue instead.'

The mother rabbit rolls her small pink eyes anxiously in our direction, and then I see her shifting position in the straw so that her body is between us and the young one.

'Come round the other side,' my mother says. 'The silly thing has moved. I do believe she's trying to hide her baby from us.'

We go round the other side of the cage. The rabbit follows us with her eyes. A couple of yards away the buck is prancing madly up and down, clawing at the wire.

'Why is Napoleon so excited?' I ask.

'I don't know, dear. Don't you bother about him. Watch Josephine. I expect she'll be having another one soon. Look how carefully she's washing that little baby! She's treating it just like a human mother treats hers! Isn't it funny to think that I did almost exactly the same sort of thing to you once?' The big blue doe is still watching us, and now, again, she pushes the baby away with her nose and rolls slowly over to face the other way. Then she goes on with her licking and cleaning.

'Isn't it wonderful how a mother knows instinctively just what she has to do?' my mother says. 'Now you just imagine, my pet, that the baby is *you*, and Josephine is *me* – wait a minute, come back over here again so you can get a better look.'

We creep back around the cage to keep the baby in view.

'See how she's fondling it and kissing it all over! There! She's *really* kissing it now, isn't she! Exactly like me and you!'

I peer closer. It seems a queer way of kissing to me.

'Look!' I scream. 'She's eating it!'

And sure enough, the head of the baby rabbit is now disappearing swiftly into the mother's mouth.

'Mummy! Quick!'

But almost before the sound of my scream has died away, the whole of that tiny pink body has vanished down the mother's throat.

I swing quickly around, and the next thing I know I'm looking straight into my mother's face, not six inches above me, and no doubt she is trying to say something or it may be that she is too astonished to say anything, but all I see is the mouth, the huge red mouth opening wider and wider until it is just a great big round gaping hole with a black centre, and I scream again, and this time I can't stop. Then suddenly out come her hands, and I can feel her skin touching mine, the long cold fingers closing tightly over my fists, and I jump back and jerk myself free and rush blindly out into the night. I run down the drive and through the front gates, screaming all the way, and then, above the noise of my own voice I can hear the jingle of bracelets coming up behind me in the dark, getting louder and louder as she keeps gaining on me all the way down the long hill to the bottom of the lane and over the bridge on to the main road where the cars are streaming by at sixty miles an hour with headlights blazing.

Then somewhere behind me I hear a screech of tyres skidding on the road surface, and then there is silence, and I notice suddenly that the bracelets aren't jingling behind me any more.

Poor Mother.

If only she could have lived a little longer.

I admit that she gave me a nasty fright with those rabbits, but it wasn't her fault, and anyway queer things like that were always happening between her and me. I had come to regard them as a sort of toughening process that did me more good than harm. But if only she could have lived long enough to complete my education, I'm sure I should never have had all that trouble I was telling you about a few minutes ago.

I want to get on with that now. I didn't mean to begin talking about my mother. She doesn't have anything to do with what I originally started out to say. I won't mention her again.

I was telling you about the spinsters in my parish. It's an ugly word, isn't it – spinster? It conjures up the vision either of a stringy old hen with a puckered mouth or of a huge ribald monster shouting around the house in riding-breeches. But these were not like that at all. They were a clean, healthy, well-built group of females, the majority of them highly bred and surprisingly wealthy, and I feel sure that the average unmarried man would have been gratified to have them around.

In the beginning, when I first came to the vicarage, I didn't have too bad a time. I enjoyed a measure of protection, of course, by reason of my calling and my cloth. In addition, I myself adopted a cool dignified attitude that was calculated to discourage familiarity. For a few months, therefore, I was able to move freely among my parishioners, and no one took the liberty of linking her arm in mine at a charity bazaar, or of touching my fingers with hers as she passed me the cruet at suppertime. I was very happy. I was feeling better than I had in years. Even that little nervous habit I had of flicking my earlobe with my forefinger when I talked began to disappear.

This was what I call my first period, and it extended over approximately six months. Then came trouble.

I suppose I should have known that a healthy male like myself couldn't hope to evade embroilment indefinitely simply by keeping a fair distance between himself and the ladies. It just doesn't work. If anything it has the opposite effect.

I would see them eyeing me covertly across the room at a whist drive, whispering to one another, nodding, running their tongues over their lips, sucking at their cigarettes, plotting the best approach, but always whispering, and sometimes I overheard snatches of their talk – 'What a shy person ... he's just a trifle nervous, isn't he ... he's much too tense ... he needs companionship ... he wants loosening up ... we must teach him how to relax.' And then slowly, as the weeks went by, they began to stalk me. I knew they were doing it. I could feel it happening although at first they did nothing definite to give themselves away.

That was my second period. It lasted for the best part of a year and was very trying indeed. But it was paradise compared with the third and final phase.

For now, instead of sniping at me sporadically from far away, the attackers suddenly came charging out of the wood with bayonets fixed. It was terrible, frightening. Nothing is more calculated to unnerve a man than the swift unexpected assault. Yet I am not a coward. I will stand my ground against any single individual of my own size under any circumstances. But this onslaught, I am now convinced, was conducted by vast numbers operating as one skilfully coordinated unit.

The first offender was Miss Elphinstone, a large woman with moles. I had dropped in on her during the afternoon to solicit a contribution towards a new set of bellows for the organ, and after some pleasant conversation in the library she had graciously handed me a cheque for two guineas. I told her not

to bother to see me to the door and I went out into the hall to
get my hat. I was about to reach for it when all at once – she
must have come tip-toeing up behind me – all at once I felt a
bare arm sliding through mine, and one second later her fingers
were entwined in my own, and she was squeezing my hand
hard, in out, in out, as though it were the bulb of a throat-spray.

'Are you really so Very Reverend as you're always pretending to be?' she whispered.

Well!

All I can tell you is that when that arm of hers came sliding
in under mine, it felt exactly as though a cobra was coiling itself
around my wrist. I leaped away, pulled open the front door,
and fled down the drive without looking back.

The very next day we held a jumble sale in the village hall
(again to raise money for the new bellows), and towards the
end of it I was standing in a corner quietly drinking a cup of
tea and keeping an eye on the villagers crowding round the
stalls when all of a sudden I heard a voice beside me saying,
'Dear me, what a hungry look you have in those eyes of yours.'
The next instant a long curvaceous body was leaning up against
mine and a hand with red fingernails was trying to push a thick
slice of coconut cake into my mouth.

'Miss Prattley,' I cried. 'Please!'

But she'd got me up against the wall, and with a teacup in
one hand and a saucer in the other I was powerless to resist. I
felt the sweat breaking out all over me and if my mouth hadn't
quickly become full of the cake she was pushing into it, I
honestly believe I would have started to scream.

A nasty incident, that one; but there was worse to come.

The next day it was Miss Unwin. Now Miss Unwin happened to be a close friend of Miss Elphinstone's *and* of Miss
Prattley's, and this of course should have been enough to make
me very cautious. Yet who would have thought that she of all
people, Miss Unwin, that quiet gentle little mouse who only a
few weeks before had presented me with a new hassock ex-
quisitely worked in needlepoint with her own hands, who
would have thought that *she* would ever have taken a liberty
with anyone? So when she asked me to accompany her down

to the crypt to show her the Saxon murals, it never entered my head that there was devilry afoot. But there was.

I don't propose to describe that encounter; it was too painful. And the ones which followed were no less savage. Nearly every day from then on, some new outrageous incident would take place. I became a nervous wreck. At times I hardly knew what I was doing. I started reading the burial service at young Gladys Pitcher's wedding. I dropped Mrs Harris's new baby into the font during the christening and gave it a nasty ducking. An uncomfortable rash that I hadn't had in over two years reappeared on the side of my neck, and that annoying business with my earlobe came back worse than ever before. Even my hair began coming out in my comb. The faster I retreated, the faster they came after me. Women are like that. Nothing stimulates them quite so much as a display of modesty or shyness in a man. And they become doubly persistent if underneath it all they happen to detect – and here I have a most difficult confession to make – if they happen to detect, as they did in me, a little secret gleam of longing shining in the backs of the eyes.

You see, actually I was mad about women.

Yes, I know. You will find this hard to believe after all that I have said, but it was perfectly true. You must understand that it was only when they touched me with their fingers or pushed up against me with their bodies that I became alarmed. Providing they remained at a safe distance, I could watch them for hours on end with the same peculiar fascination that you yourself might experience in watching a creature you couldn't bear to touch – an octopus, for example, or a long poisonous snake. I loved the smooth white look of a bare arm emerging from a sleeve, curiously naked like a peeled banana. I could get enormously excited just from watching a girl walk across the room in a tight dress; and I particularly enjoyed the back view of a pair of legs when the feet were in rather high heels – the wonderful braced-up look behind the knees, with the legs themselves very taut as though they were made of strong elastic stretched out almost to breaking-point, but not quite. Sometimes, in Lady Birdwell's drawing-room, sitting near the window on a summer's afternoon, I would glance over the rim of my teacup towards the swimming pool and become agitated beyond measure by the sight of a little patch of sunburned stomach bulging between the top and bottom of a two-piece bathing-suit.

There is nothing wrong in having thoughts like these. All men harbour them from time to time. But they did give me a terrible sense of guilt. Is it me, I kept asking myself, who is unwittingly responsible for the shameless way in which these ladies are now behaving? Is it the gleam in my eye (which I cannot control) that is constantly rousing their passions and egging them on? Am I unconsciously giving them what is sometimes known as the come-hither signal every time I glance their way? Am I?

Or is this brutal conduct of theirs inherent in the very nature of the female?

I had a pretty fair idea of the answer to this question, but that was not good enough for me. I happen to possess a con-science that can never be consoled by guesswork; it has to have proof. I simply had to find out who was really the guilty party in this case – me or them, and with this object in view, I now decided to perform a simple experiment of my own invention, using Snelling's rats.

A year or so previously I had had some trouble with an objectionable choirboy named Billy Snelling. On three consecu-tive Sundays this youth had brought a pair of white rats into church and had let them loose on the floor during my sermon. In the end I had confiscated the animals and carried them home and placed them in a box in the shed at the bottom of the vicarage garden. Purely for humane reasons I had then pro-ceeded to feed them, and as a result, but without any further encouragement from me, the creatures began to multiply very rapidly. The two became five, and the five became twelve.

It was at this point that I decided to use them for research purposes. There were exactly equal numbers of males and females, six of each, so that conditions were ideal.

I first isolated the sexes, putting them into two separate cages, and I left them like that for three whole weeks. Now a rat is a very lascivious animal, and any zoologist will tell you that for them this is an inordinately long period of separation. At a guess I would say that one week of enforced celibacy for a rat is equal to approximately one year of the same treatment for someone like Miss Elphinstone or Miss Prattley; so you can see that I was doing a pretty fair job in reproducing actual conditions.

When the three weeks were up, I took a large box that was divided across the centre by a little fence, and I placed the females on one side and the males on the other. The fence consisted of nothing more than three single strands of naked wire, one inch apart, but there was a powerful electric current running through the wires.

To add a touch of reality to the proceedings, I gave each female a name. The largest one, who also had the longest whiskers, was Miss Elphinstone. The one with a short thick tail was Miss Prattley. The smallest of them all was Miss Unwin, and so on. The males, all six of them, were ME.

I now pulled up a chair and sat back to watch the result.

All rats are suspicious by nature, and when I first put the two sexes together in the box with only the wire between them, neither side made a move. The males stared hard at the females through the fence. The females stared back, waiting for the males to come forward. I could see that both sides were tense with yearning. Whiskers quivered and noses twitched and occasionally a long tail would flick sharply against the wall of the box.

After a while, the first male detached himself from his group and advanced gingerly towards the fence, his belly close to the ground. He touched a wire and was immediately electrocuted. The remaining eleven rats froze, motionless.

There followed a period of nine and a half minutes during which neither side moved; but I noticed that while all the males were now staring at the dead body of their colleague, the females had eyes only for the males.

Then suddenly Miss Prattley with the short tail could stand it no longer. She came bounding forward, hit the wire, and dropped dead.

The males pressed their bodies closer to the ground and gazed thoughtfully at the two corpses by the fence. The females also seemed to be quite shaken, and there was another wait, with neither side moving.

Now it was Miss Unwin who began to show signs of impatience. She snorted audibly and twitched a pink mobile nose-end from side to side, then suddenly she started jerking her body quickly up and down as though she were doing pushups. She glanced round at her remaining four companions, raised her tail high in the air as much as to say, 'Here I go, girls,' and with that she advanced briskly to the wire, pushed her head through it, and was killed.

Sixteen minutes later, Miss Foster made her first move. Miss Foster was a woman in the village who bred cats, and recently she had had the effrontery to put up a large sign outside her house in the High Street, saying FOSTER'S CATTERY. Through long association with the creatures she herself seemed to have acquired all their most noxious characteristics, and whenever she came near me in a room I could detect, even through the smoke of her Russian cigarette, a faint but pungent aroma of cat. She had never struck me as having much control over her baser instincts, and it was with some satisfaction, therefore, that I watched her now as she foolishly took her own life in a last desperate plunge towards the masculine sex.

A Miss Montgomery-Smith came next, a small determined woman who had once tried to make me believe that she had been engaged to a bishop. She died trying to creep on her belly under the lowest wire, and I must say I thought this a very fair reflection upon the way in which she lived her life.

And still the five remaining males stayed motionless, waiting.

The fifth female to go was Miss Plumley. She was a devious one who was continually slipping little messages addressed to me into the collection bag. Only the Sunday before, I had been in the vestry counting the money after morning service and had comes across one of them tucked inside a folded ten-shilling note. *Your poor throat sounded hoarse today during the sermon,* it said. *Let me bring you a bottle of my own cherry pectoral to soothe it down. Most affectionately, Eunice Plumley.*

Miss Plumley ambled slowly up to the wire, sniffed the centre strand with the tip of her nose, came a fraction too close, and received two hundred and forty volts of alternating current through her body.

The five males stayed where they were, watching the slaughter.

And now only Miss Elphinstone remained on the feminine side.

For a full half-hour neither she nor any of the others made a move. Finally one of the males stirred himself slightly, took a step forward, hesitated, thought better of it, and slowly sank back into a crouch on the floor.

This must have frustrated Miss Elphinstone beyond measure, for suddenly, with eyes blazing, she rushed forward and took a flying leap at the wire. It was a spectacular jump and she nearly cleared it, but one of her hind legs grazed the top strand, and thus she also perished with the rest of her sex.

I cannot tell you how much good it did me to watch this simple and, though I say it myself, this rather ingenious experiment. In one stroke I had laid open the incredibly lascivious, stop-at-nothing nature of the female. My own sex was vindicated; my own conscience was cleared. In a trice, all those awkward little flashes of guilt from which I had continually been suffering flew out of the window. I felt suddenly very strong and serene in the knowledge of my own innocence.

For a few moments I toyed with the absurd idea of electrifying the black iron railings that ran around the vicarage garden; or perhaps just the gate would be enough. Then I would sit back comfortably in a chair in the library and watch through the window as the real Misses Elphinstone and Prattley and Unwin came forward one after the other and paid the final penalty for pestering an innocent male.

Such foolish thoughts!

What I must actually do now, I told myself, was to weave around me a sort of invisible electric fence constructed entirely out of my own personal moral fibre. Behind this I would sit in perfect safety while the enemy, one after another, flung themselves against the wire.

I would begin by cultivating a brusque manner. I would speak crisply to all women, and refrain from smiling at them. I would no longer step back a pace when one of them advanced upon me. I would stand my ground and glare at her, and if she said something that I considered suggestive, I would make a sharp retort.

It was in this mood that I set off the very next day to attend Lady Birdwell's tennis party.

I was not a player myself, but her ladyship had graciously invited me to drop in and mingle with the guests when play was over at six o'clock. I believe she thought that it lent a certain tone to a gathering to have a clergyman present, and she was probably hoping to persuade me to repeat the performance I gave the last time I was there, when I sat at the piano for a full hour and a quarter after supper and entertained the guests with a detailed description of the evolution of the madrigal through the centuries.

I arrived at the gates on my cycle promptly at six o'clock and pedalled up the long drive towards the house. This was the first week of June, and the rhododendrons were massed in great banks of pink and purple all the way along on either side. I was feeling unusually blithe and dauntless. The previous day's experiment with rats had made it impossible now for anyone to take me by surprise. I knew exactly what to expect and I was armed accordingly. All around me the little fence was up.

'Ah, good evening, Vicar,' Lady Birdwell cried, advancing upon me with both arms outstretched.

I stood my ground and looked her straight in the eyes. 'How's Birdwell?' I said. 'Still up in the city?'

I doubt whether she had ever before in her life heard Lord Birdwell referred to thus by someone who had never even met him. It stopped her dead in her tracks. She looked at me queerly and didn't seem to know how to answer.

'I'll take a seat if I may,' I said, and walked past her towards the terrace where a group of nine or ten guests were settled comfortably in cane chairs, sipping their drinks. They were mostly women, the usual crowd, all of them dressed in white tennis clothes, and as I strode in among them my own sober black suiting seemed to give me, I thought, just the right amount of separateness for the occasion.

The ladies greeted me with smiles. I nodded to them and sat down in a vacant chair, but I didn't smile back.

'I think perhaps I'd better finish my story another time,' Miss Elphinstone was saying. 'I don't believe the vicar would approve.' She giggled and gave me an arch look. I knew she was waiting for me to come out with my usual little nervous laugh and to say my usual little sentence about how broadminded I was; but I did nothing of the sort. I simply raised one side of my upper lip until it shaped itself into a tiny curl of contempt (I had practised in the mirror that morning), and then I said sharply, in a loud voice, *Mens sana in corpore sano.*

'What's that?' she cried. 'Come again, Vicar.'

'A clean mind in a healthy body,' I answered. 'It's a family motto.'

There was an odd kind of silence for quite a long time after this. I could see the women exchanging glances with one another, frowning, shaking their heads.

'The vicar's in the dumps,' Miss Foster announced. She was the one who bred cats. 'I think the vicar needs a drink.'

'Thank you,' I said, 'but I never imbibe. You know that.'

'Then do let me fetch you a nice cooling glass of fruit cup?'

This last sentence came softly and rather suddenly from someone just behind me, to my right, and there was a note of such genuine concern in the speaker's voice that I turned round.

I saw a lady of singular beauty whom I had met only once before, about a month ago. Her name was Miss Roach, and I remembered that she had struck me then as being a person far out of the usual run. I had been particularly impressed by her gentle and reticent nature; and the fact that I had felt comfortable in her presence proved beyond doubt that she was not the sort of person who would try to impinge herself upon me in any way.

'I'm sure you must be tired after cycling all that distance,' she was saying now.

I swivelled right round in my chair and looked at her carefully. She was certainly a striking person – unusually muscular for a woman, with broad shoulders and powerful arms and a huge calf bulging on each leg. The flush of the afternoon's exertions was still upon her, and her face glowed with a healthy red sheen.

49

'Thank you so much, Miss Roach,' I said, 'but I never touch alcohol in any form. Maybe a small glass of lemon squash . . .'

'The fruit cup is only made of fruit, Padre.'

How I loved a person who called me 'Padre'. The word has a military ring about it that conjures up visions of stern discipline and officer rank.

'Fruit cup?' Miss Elphinstone said. 'It's harmless.'

'My dear man, it's nothing but vitamin C,' Miss Foster said.

'Much beter for you than fizzy lemonade,' Lady Birdwell said. 'Carbon dioxide attacks the lining of the stomach.'

'I'll get you some,' Miss Roach said, smiling at me pleasantly. It was a good open smile, and there wasn't a trace of guile or mischief from one corner of the mouth to the other.

She stood up and walked over to the drink table. I saw her slicing an orange, then an apple, then a cucumber, then a grape, and dropping the pieces into a glass. Then she poured in a large quantity of liquid from a bottle whose label I couldn't quite read without my spectacles, but I fancied that I saw the name JIM on it, or TIM, or PIM, or some such word.

'I hope there's enough left,' Lady Birdwell called out. 'Those greedy children of mine do love it so.'

'Plenty,' Miss Roach answered, and she brought the drink to me and set it on the table.

Even without tasting it I could easily understand why children adored it. The liquid itself was dark amber-red and there were great hunks of fruit floating around among the ice cubes; and on top of it all, Miss Roach had placed a sprig of mint. I guessed that the mint had been put there specially for me, to take some of the sweetness away and to lend a touch of grown-upness to a concoction that was otherwise so obviously for youngsters.

'Too sticky for you, Padre!'

'It's delectable,' I said, sipping it. 'Quite perfect.'

It seemed a pity to gulp it down quickly after all the trouble Miss Roach had taken to make it, but it was so refreshing I couldn't resist.

'Do let me make you another!'

I liked the way she waited until I had set the glass on the table, instead of trying to take it out of my hand.

'I wouldn't eat the mint if I were you,' Miss Elphinstone said.

'I'd better get another bottle from the house,' Lady Birdwell called out. 'You're going to need it, Mildred.'

'Do that,' Miss Roach replied. 'I drink gallons of the stuff myself,' she went on, speaking to me. 'And I don't think you'd say that I'm exactly what you might call emaciated.'

'No indeed,' I answered fervently. I was watching her again as she mixed me another brew, noticing how the muscles rippled under the skin of the arm that raised the bottle. Her neck also was uncommonly fine when seen from behind; not thin and stringy like the necks of a lot of these so-called modern beauties, but thick and strong with a slight ridge running down either side where the sinews bulged. It wasn't easy to guess the age of a person like this, but I doubted whether she could have been more than forty-eight or nine.

I had just finished my second big glass of fruit cup when I began to experience a most peculiar sensation. I seemed to be floating up out of my chair, and hundreds of little warm waves came washing in under me, lifting me higher and higher. I felt as buoyant as a bubble, and everything around me seemed to be bobbing up and down and swirling gently from side to side. It was all very pleasant, and I was overcome by an almost irresistible desire to break into song.

'Feeling happy?' Miss Roach's voice sounded miles and miles away, and when I turned to look at her, I was astonished to see how near she really was. She, also, was bobbing up and down.

'Terrific,' I answered. 'I'm feeling absolutely terrific.'

Her face was large and pink, and it was so close to me now that I could see the pale carpet of fuzz covering both her cheeks, and the way the sunlight caught each tiny separate hair and made it shine like gold. All of a sudden I found myself wanting to put out a hand and stroke those cheeks of hers with my fingers. To tell the truth, I wouldn't have objected in the least if she had tried to do the same to me.

'Listen,' she said softly. 'How about the two of us taking a little stroll down the garden to see the lupins?'

'Fine,' I answered. 'Lovely. Anything you say.'

There is a small Georgian summer-house alongside the

croquet lawn in Lady Birdwell's garden, and the very next thing I knew, I was sitting inside it on a kind of chaise-longue and Miss Roach was beside me. I was still bobbing up and down, and so was she, and so, for that matter, was the summer-house, but I was feeling wonderful. I asked Miss Roach if she would like me to give her a song.

'Not now,' she said, encircling me with her arms and squeezing my chest against hers so hard that it hurt.

'Don't,' I said, melting.

'That's better,' she kept saying. 'That's much better, isn't it?'

Had Miss Roach or any other female tried to do this sort of thing to me an hour before, I don't quite know what would have happened. I think I would probably have fainted. I might even have died. But here I was now, the same old me, actually relishing the contact of those enormous bare arms against my body! Also – and this was the most amazing thing of all – I was beginning to feel the urge to reciprocate.

I took the lobe of her left ear between my thumb and forefinger, and tugged it playfully.

'Naughty boy,' she said.

I tugged harder and squeezed it a bit at the same time. This roused her to such a pitch that she began to grunt and snort like a hog. Her breathing became loud and stertorous.

'Kiss me,' she ordered.

'What?' I said.

'Come on, kiss me.'

At that moment, I saw her mouth. I saw this great mouth of hers coming slowly down on top of me, starting to open, and coming closer and closer, and opening wider and wider; and suddenly my whole stomach began to roll over inside me and I went stiff with terror.

'No!' I shrieked. 'Don't! Don't, Mummy, don't!'

I can only tell you that I had never in all my life seen anything more terrifying than that mouth. I simply could not *stand* it coming at me like that. Had it been a red-hot iron someone was pushing into my face I wouldn't have been nearly so petrified, I swear I wouldn't. The strong arms were around me, pinning me down so that I couldn't move, and the mouth kept getting larger and larger, and then all at once it was right on

top of me, huge and wet and cavernous, and the next second –
I was inside it.

I was right inside this enormous mouth, lying on my stomach
along the length of the tongue, with my feet somewhere around
the back of the throat; and I knew instinctively that unless I got
myself out again at once I was going to be swallowed alive –
just like that baby rabbit. I could feel my legs being drawn
down the throat by some kind of suction, and quickly I threw
up my arms and grabbed hold of the lower front teeth and held
on for dear life. My head was near the mouth-entrance, and I
could actually look right out between the lips and see a little
patch of the world outside – sunlight shining on the polished
wooden floor of the summer-house, and on the floor itself a
gigantic foot in a white tennis shoe.

I had a good grip with my fingers on the edge of the teeth,
and in spite of the suction, I was managing to haul myself up
slowly towards the daylight when suddenly the upper teeth
came down on my knuckles and started chopping away at them
so fiercely I had to let go. I went sliding back down the throat,
feet first, clutching madly at this and that as I went, but everything was so smooth and slippery I couldn't get a grip. I
glimpsed a bright flash of gold on the left as I slid past the last
of the molars, and then three inches farther on I saw what must
have been the uvula above me, dangling like a thick red stalac-
tite from the roof of the throat. I grabbed at it with both hands
but the thing slithered through my fingers and I went on down.

I remember screaming for help, but I could barely hear the
sound of my own voice above the noise of the wind that was
caused by the throat-owner's breathing. There seemed to be a
gale blowing all the time, a queer erratic gale that blew altern-
ately very cold (as the air came in) and very hot (as it went out
again).

I managed to get my elbows hooked over a sharp fleshy
ridge – I presume the epiglottis – and for a brief moment I hung
there, defying the suction and scrabbling with my feet to find a
foothold on the wall of the larynx; but the throat gave a huge
swallow that jerked me away, and down I went again.

From then on, there was nothing else for me to catch hold
of, and down and down I went until soon my legs were dangling

below me in the upper reaches of the stomach, and I could feel the slow powerful pulsing of peristalsis dragging away at my ankles, pulling me down and down and down ...

Far above me, outside in the open air, I could hear the distant babble of women's voices:

'It's not true ...'

'But my dear Mildred, how awful ...'

'The man must be mad ...'

'Your poor mouth, just look at it ...'

'A sex maniac ...'

'A sadist ...'

'Someone ought to write to the bishop ...'

And then Miss Roach's voice, louder than the others, swearing and screeching like a parakeet:

'He's damn lucky I didn't kill him, the little bastard! ... I said to him, listen, I said, if ever I happen to want any of my teeth extracted, I'll go to a dentist, not to a goddamn vicar ... It isn't as though I'd given him any encouragement either! ...'

'Where is he now, Mildred?'

'God knows. In the bloody summer-house, I suppose.'

'Hey girls, let's go and root him out!'

Oh dear, oh dear. Looking back on it all now, some three weeks later, I don't know how I ever came through the nightmare of that awful afternoon without taking leave of my senses.

A gang of witches like that is a very dangerous thing to fool around with, and had they managed to catch me in the summer-house right then and there when their blood was up, they would as likely as not have torn me limb from limb on the spot.

Either that, or I should have been frog-marched down to the police station with Lady Birdwell and Miss Roach leading the procession through the main street of the village.

But of course they didn't catch me.

They didn't catch me then, and they haven't caught me yet, and if my luck continues to hold, I think I've got a fair chance of evading them altogether – or anyway for a few months, until they forget about the whole affair.

As you might guess, I am having to keep entirely to myself and to take no part in public affairs or social life. I find that writing is a most salutary occupation at a time like this, and I spend many hours each day playing with sentences. I regard each sentence as a little wheel, and my ambition lately has been to gather several hundred of them together at once and to fit them all end to end, with the cogs interlocking, like gears, but each wheel a different size, each turning at a different speed. Now and again I try to put a really big one right next to a very small one in such a way that the big one, turning slowly, will make the small one spin so fast that it hums. Very tricky, that.

I also sing madrigals in the evenings, but I miss my own harpsichord terribly.

All the same, this isn't such a bad place, and I have made myself as comfortable as I possibly can. It is a small chamber situated in what is almost certainly the primary section of the duodenal loop, just before it begins to run vertically downward in front of the right kidney. The floor is quite level – indeed it was the first level place I came to during that horrible descent down Miss Roach's throat – and that's the only reason I managed to stop at all. Above me, I can see a pulpy sort of opening that I take to be the pylorus, where the stomach enters the small intestine (I can still remember some of those diagrams my mother used to show me), and below me, there is a funny little hole in the wall where the pancreatic duct enters the lower section of the duodenum.

It is all a trifle bizarre for a man of conservative tastes like myself. Personally I prefer oak furniture and parquet flooring. But there is anyway one thing here that pleases me greatly, and that is the walls. They are lovely and soft, like a sort of padding, and the advantage of this is that I can bounce up against them as much as I wish without hurting myself.

There are several other people about, which is rather surprising, but thank God they are every one of them males. For some reason or other, they all wear white coats, and they bustle around pretending to be very busy and important. In actual fact, they are an uncommonly ignorant bunch of fellows. They don't even seem to realize who they *are*. I try to tell them, but they refuse to listen. Sometimes I get so angry and frustrated with them that I lose my temper and start to shout; and then

a sly mistrustful look comes over their faces and they begin
backing slowly away, and saying, 'Now then. Take it easy. Take
it easy, Vicar, there's a good boy. Take it easy.'

What sort of talk is that?

But there is one oldish man – he comes in to see me every
morning after breakfast – who appears to live slightly closer to
reality than the others. He is civil and dignified, and I imagine
he is lonely because he likes nothing better than to sit quietly in
my room and listen to me talk. The only trouble is that whenever we get on the subject of our whereabouts, he starts telling
me that he's going to help me to escape. He said it again this
morning, and we had quite an argument about it.

'But can't you see,' I said patiently, 'I don't *want* to escape.'

'My dear Vicar, why ever not?'

'I keep telling you – because they're all searching for me
outside.'

'Who?'

'Miss Elphinstone and Miss Roach and Miss Prattley and all
the rest of them.'

'What nonsense.'

'Oh yes they are! And I imagine they're after *you* as well,
but you won't admit it.'

'No, my friend, they are not after me.'

'Then may I ask precisely what you are doing down here?'

A bit of a stumper for him, that one. I could see he didn't
know how to answer it.

'I'll bet you were fooling around with Miss Roach and got
yourself swallowed up just the same as I did. I'll bet that's
exactly what happened, only you're ashamed to admit it.'

He looked suddenly so wan and defeated when I said this
that I felt sorry for him.

'Would you like me to sing you a song?' I asked.

But he got up without answering and went quietly out into
the corridor.

'Cheer up,' I called after him. 'Don't be depressed. There is
always some balm in Gilead.'

# Genesis and Catastrophe

## A TRUE STORY

'Everything is normal,' the doctor was saying. 'Just lie back and relax.' His voice was miles away in the distance and he seemed to be shouting at her. 'You have a son.'

'What?'

'You have a fine son. You understand that, don't you? A fine son. Did you hear him crying?'

'Is he all right, Doctor?'

'Of course he is all right.'

'Please let me see him.'

'You'll see him in a moment.'

'You are certain he is all right?'

'I am quite certain.'

'Is he still crying?'

'Try to rest. There is nothing to worry about.'

'Why has he stopped crying, Doctor? What happened?'

'Don't excite yourself, please. Everything is normal.'

'I want to see him. Please let me see him.'

'Dear lady,' the doctor said, patting her hand. 'You have a fine strong healthy child. Don't you believe me when I tell you that?'

'What is the woman over there doing to him?'

'Your baby is being made to look pretty for you,' the doctor said. 'We are giving him a little wash, that is all. You must spare us a moment or two for that.'

'You swear he is all right?'

'I swear it. Now lie back and relax. Close your eyes. Go on, close your eyes. That's right. That's better. Good girl . . .'

'I have prayed and prayed that he will live, Doctor.'

'Of course he will live. What are you talking about?'

'The others didn't.'

'What?'

'None of my other ones lived, Doctor.'

The doctor stood beside the bed looking down at the pale exhausted face of the young woman. He had never seen her before today. She and her husband were new people in the town. The innkeeper's wife, who had come up to assist in the delivery, had told him that the husband worked at the local customs-house on the border and that the two of them had arrived quite suddenly at the inn with one trunk and one suitcase about three months ago. The husband was a drunkard, the innkeeper's wife had said, an arrogant, overbearing, bullying little drunkard, but the young woman was gentle and religious. And she was very sad. She never smiled. In the few weeks that she had been here, the innkeeper's wife had never once seen her smile. Also there was a rumour that this was the husband's third marriage, that one wife had died and that the other had divorced him for unsavoury reasons. But that was only a rumour.

The doctor bent down and pulled the sheet up a little higher over the patient's chest. 'You have nothing to worry about,' he said gently. 'This is a perfectly normal baby.'

'That's exactly what they told me about the others. But I lost them all, Doctor. In the last eighteen months I have lost all three of my children, so you mustn't blame me for being anxious.'

'Three?'

'This is my fourth ... in four years.'

The doctor shifted his feet uneasily on the bare floor.

'I don't think you know what it means, Doctor, to lose them all, all three of them, slowly, separately, one by one. I keep seeing them. I can see Gustav's face now as clearly as if he were lying here beside me in the bed. Gustav was a lovely boy, Doctor. But he was always ill. It is terrible when they are always ill and there is nothing you can do to help them.'

'I know.'

The woman opened her eyes, stared up at the doctor for a few seconds, then closed them again.

'My little girl was called Ida. She died a few days before Christmas. That is only four months ago. I just wish you could have seen Ida, Doctor.'

'You have a new one now.'

'But Ida was so beautiful.'

'Yes,' the doctor said. 'I know.'

'How can you know?' she cried.

'I am sure that she was a lovely child. But this new one is also like that.' The doctor turned away from the bed and walked over to the window and stood there looking out. It was a wet grey April afternoon, and across the street he could see the red roofs of the houses and the huge raindrops splashing on the tiles.

'Ida was two years old, Doctor . . . and she was so beautiful I was never able to take my eyes off her from the time I dressed her in the morning until she was safe in bed again at night. I used to live in holy terror of something happening to that child. Gustav had gone and my little Otto had also gone and she was all I had left. Sometimes I used to get up in the night and creep over to the cradle and put my ear close to her mouth just to make sure that she was breathing.'

'Try to rest,' the doctor said, going back to the bed. 'Please try to rest.' The woman's face was white and bloodless, and there was a slight bluish-grey tinge around the nostrils and the mouth. A few strands of damp hair hung down over her forehead, sticking to the skin.

'When she died . . . I was already pregnant again when that happened, Doctor. This new one was a good four months on its way when Ida died. "I don't want it!" I shouted after the funeral. "I won't have it! I have buried enough children!" And my husband . . . he was strolling among the guests with a big glass of beer in his hand . . . he turned around quickly and said, "I have news for you, Klara, I have good news." Can you imagine that, Doctor? We have just buried our third child and he stands there with a glass of beer in his hand and tells me that he has good news. "Today I have been posted to Braunau," he says, "so you can start packing at once. This will be a new start for you, Klara," he says. "It will be a new place and you can have a new doctor . . ." '

'Please don't talk any more.'

'You *are* the new doctor, aren't you, Doctor?'

'That's right.'

'And here we are in Braunau.'

'Yes.'

'I am frightened, Doctor.'

'Try not to be frightened.'

'What chance can the fourth one have now?'

'You must stop thinking like that.'

'I can't help it. I am certain there is something inherited that causes my children to die in this way. There must be.'

'That is nonsense.'

'Do you know what my husband said to me when Otto was born, Doctor? He came into the room and he looked into the cradle where Otto was lying and he said, "Why do *all* my children have to be so small and weak?"'

'I am sure he didn't say that.'

'He put his head right into Otto's cradle as though he were examining a tiny insect and he said, "All I am saying is why can't they be better *specimens*? That's all I am saying." And three days after that, Otto was dead. We baptized him quickly on the third day and he died the same evening. And then Gustav died. And then Ida died. All of them died, Doctor . . . and suddenly the whole house was empty . . .'

'Don't think about it now.'

'Is this one so very small?'

'He is a normal child.'

'But small?'

'He is a little small, perhaps. But the small ones are often a lot tougher than the big ones. Just imagine, Frau Hitler, this time next year he will be almost learning how to walk. Isn't that a lovely thought?'

She didn't answer this.

'And two years from now he will probably be talking his head off and driving you crazy with his chatter. Have you settled on a name for him yet?'

'A name?'

'Yes.'

'I don't know. I'm not sure. I think my husband said that if it was a boy we were going to call him Adolfus.'

'That means he would be called Adolf.'

'Yes. My husband likes Adolf because it has a certain similarity to Alois. My husband is called Alois.'

'Excellent.'

'Oh no!' she cried, starting up suddenly from the pillow. 'That's the same question they asked me when Otto was born! It means he is going to die! You are going to baptize him at once!'

'Now, now,' the doctor said, taking her gently by the shoulders. 'You are quite wrong. I promise you you are wrong. I was simply being an inquisitive old man, that is all. I love talking about names. I think Adolphus is a particularly fine name. It is one of my favourites. And look – here he comes now.'

The innkeeper's wife, carrying the baby high up on her enormous bosom, came sailing across the room towards the bed. 'Here is the little beauty!' she cried, beaming. 'Would you like to hold him, my dear? Shall I put him beside you?'

'Is he well wrapped?' the doctor asked. 'It is extremely cold in here.'

'Certainly he is well wrapped.'

The baby was tightly swaddled in a white woollen shawl, and only the tiny pink head protruded. The innkeeper's wife placed him gently on the bed beside the mother. 'There you are,' she said. 'Now you can lie there and look at him to your heart's content.'

'I think you will like him,' the doctor said, smiling. 'He is a fine little baby.'

'He has the most lovely hands!' the innkeeper's wife exclaimed. 'Such long delicate fingers!'

The mother didn't move. She didn't even turn her head to look.

'Go on!' cried the innkeeper's wife. 'He won't bite you!'

'I am frightened to look. I don't dare to believe that I have another baby and that he is all right.'

'Don't be so stupid.'

Slowly, the mother turned her head and looked at the small, incredibly serene face that lay on the pillow beside her.

'Is this my baby?'

'Of course.'

'Oh ... oh ... but he is beautiful.'

The doctor turned away and went over to the table and began putting his things into his bag. The mother lay on the bed gazing at the child and smiling and touching him and making little noises of pleasure. 'Hello, Adolfus,' she whispered. 'Hello, my little Adolf ...'

'Ssshh!' said the innkeeper's wife. 'Listen! I think your husband is coming.'

The doctor walked over to the door and opened it and looked out into the corridor.

'Herr Hitler!'

'Yes.'

'Come in, please.'

A small man in a dark-green uniform stepped softly into the room and looked around him.

'Congratulations,' the doctor said. 'You have a son.'

The man had a pair of enormous whiskers meticulously groomed after the manner of the Emperor Franz Josef, and he smelled strongly of beer. 'A son?'

'Yes.'

'How is he?'

'He is fine. So is your wife.'

'Good.' The father turned and walked with a curious little prancing stride over to the bed where his wife was lying. 'Well, Klara,' he said, smiling through his whiskers. 'How did it go?' He bent down to take a look at the baby. Then he bent lower. In a series of quick jerky movements, he bent lower and lower until his face was only about twelve inches from the baby's head. The wife lay sideways on the pillow, staring up at him with a kind of supplicating look.

'He has the most marvellous pair of lungs,' the innkeeper's wife announced. 'You should have heard him screaming just after he came into this world.'

'But my God, Klara ...'

'What is it, dear?'

'This one is even smaller than Otto was!'

The doctor took a couple of quick paces forward. 'There is nothing wrong with that child,' he said.

Slowly, the husband straightened up and turned away from the bed and looked at the doctor. He seemed bewildered and stricken. 'It's no good lying, Doctor,' he said. 'I know what it means. It's going to be the same all over again.'

'Now you listen to me,' the doctor said.

'But do you *know* what happened to the others, Doctor?'

'You must forget about the others, Herr Hitler. Give this one a chance.'

'But so small and weak!'

'My dear sir, he has only just been born.'

'Even so ...'

'What are you trying to do?' cried the innkeeper's wife. 'Talk him into his grave?'

'That's enough!' the doctor said sharply.

The mother was weeping now. Great sobs were shaking her body.

The doctor walked over to the husband and put a hand on his shoulder. 'Be good to her,' he whispered. 'Please. It is very important.' Then he squeezed the husband's shoulder hard and began pushing him forward surreptitiously to the edge of the bed. The husband hesitated. The doctor squeezed harder, signalling him urgently through fingers and thumb. At last, reluctantly, the husband bent down and kissed his wife lightly on the cheek.

'All right, Klara,' he said. 'Now stop crying.'

'I have prayed so hard that he will live, Alois.'

'Yes.'

'Every day for months I have gone to the church and begged on my knees that this one will be allowed to live.'

'Yes, Klara, I know.'

'Three dead children is all that I can stand, don't you realize that?'

'Of course.'

'He *must* live, Alois. He *must*, he *must* ... Oh God, be merciful unto him now ...'

# The Hitch-hiker

I had a new car. It was an exciting toy, a big B.M.W. 3·3 Li, which means 3·3 litre, long wheelbase, fuel injection. It had a top speed of 129 m.p.h. and terrific acceleration. The body was pale blue. The seats inside were darker blue and they were made of leather, genuine soft leather of the finest quality. The windows were electrically operated and so was the sun-roof. The radio aerial popped up when I switched on the radio, and disappeared when I switched it off. The powerful engine growled and grunted impatiently at slow speeds, but at sixty miles an hour the growling stopped and the motor began to purr with pleasure.

I was driving up to London by myself. It was a lovely June day. They were haymaking in the fields and there were buttercups along both sides of the road. I was whispering along at seventy miles an hour, leaning back comfortably in my seat, with no more than a couple of fingers resting lightly on the wheel to keep her steady. Ahead of me I saw a man thumbing a lift. I touched the footbrake and brought the car to a stop beside him. I always stopped for hitch-hikers. I knew just how it used to feel to be standing on the side of a country road watching the cars go by. I hated the drivers for pretending they didn't see me, especially the ones in big cars with three empty seats. The large expensive cars seldom stopped. It was always the smaller ones that offered you a lift, or the old rusty ones, or the ones that were already crammed full of children and the driver would say, 'I think we can squeeze in one more.'

The hitch-hiker poked his head through the open window and said, 'Going to London, guv'nor?'

'Yes,' I said. 'Jump in.'

He got in and I drove on.

He was a small ratty-faced man with grey teeth. His eyes were dark and quick and clever, like a rat's eyes, and his ears were slightly pointed at the top. He had a cloth cap on his head and he was wearing a greyish-coloured jacket with enormous pockets. The grey jacket, together with the quick eyes and the pointed ears, made him look more than anything like some sort of a huge human rat.

'What part of London are you headed for?' I asked him.

'I'm goin' right through London and out the other side,' he said. 'I'm goin' to Epsom, for the races. It's Derby Day today.'

'So it is,' I said. 'I wish I were going with you. I love betting on horses.'

'I never bet on horses,' he said. 'I don't even watch 'em run. That's a stupid silly business.'

'Then why do you go?' I asked.

He didn't seem to like that question. His little ratty face went absolutely blank and he sat there staring straight ahead at the road, saying nothing.

'I expect you help to work the betting machines or something like that,' I said.

'That's even sillier,' he answered. 'There's no fun working them lousy machines and selling tickets to mugs. Any fool could do that.'

There was a long silence. I decided not to question him any more. I remembered how irritated I used to get in my hitch-hiking days when drivers kept asking *me* questions. Where are you going? Why are you going there? What's your job? Are you married? Do you have a girl-friend? What's her name? How old are you? And so on and so forth. I used to hate it.

'I'm sorry,' I said. 'It's none of my business what you do. The trouble is, I'm a writer, and most writers are terrible nosey parkers.'

'You write books?' he asked.

'Yes.'

'Writin' books is okay,' he said. 'It's what I call a skilled trade. I'm in a skilled trade too. The folks I despise is them that spend all their lives doin' crummy old routine jobs with no skill in 'em at all. You see what I mean?'

'Yes.'

'The secret of life,' he said, 'is to become very very good at somethin' that's very very 'ard to do.'

'Like you,' I said.

'Exactly. You and me both.'

'What makes you think that *I'm* any good at my job?' I asked. 'There's an awful lot of bad writers around.'

'You wouldn't be drivin' about in a car like this if you weren't no good at it,' he answered. 'It must've cost a tidy packet, this little job.'

'It wasn't cheap.'

'What can she do flat out?' he asked.

'One hundred and twenty-nine miles an hour,' I told him.

'I'll bet she won't do it.'

'I'll bet she will.'

'All car makers is liars,' he said. 'You can buy any car you like and it'll never do what the makers say it will in the ads.'

'This one will.'

'Open 'er up then and prove it,' he said. 'Go on, guv'nor, open 'er right up and let's see what she'll do.'

There is a roundabout at Chalfont St Peter and immediately beyond it there's a long straight section of dual carriageway. We came out of the roundabout on to the carriageway and I pressed my foot down on the accelerator. The big car leaped forward as though she'd been stung. In ten seconds or so, we were doing ninety.

'Lovely!' he cried. 'Beautiful! Keep goin'!'

I had the accelerator jammed right down against the floor and I held it there.

'One hundred!' he shouted ... 'A hundred and five! ... A hundred and ten! ... A hundred and fifteen! Go on! Don't slack off!'

I was in the outside lane and we flashed past several cars as though they were standing still – a green Mini, a big cream-coloured Citroën, a white Land-Rover, a huge truck with a container on the back, an orange-coloured Volkswagen Mini-bus ...

'A hundred and twenty!' my passenger shouted, jumping up and down. 'Go on! Go on! Get 'er up to one-two-nine!'

At that moment, I heard the scream of a police siren. It was so loud it seemed to be right inside the car, and then a police-

man on a motor-cycle loomed up alongside us on the inside
lane and went past us and raised a hand for us to stop.

'Oh, my sainted aunt!' I said. 'That's torn it!'

The policeman must have been doing about a hundred and
thirty when he passed us, and he took plenty of time slowing
down. Finally, he pulled into the side of the road and I pulled
in behind him. 'I didn't know police motor-cycles could go as
fast as that,' I said rather lamely.

'That one can,' my passenger said. 'It's the same make as
yours. It's a B.M.W. R90S. Fastest bike on the road. That's
what they're usin' nowadays.'

The policeman got off his motor-cycle and leaned the
machine sideways on to its prop stand. Then he took off his
gloves and placed them carefully on the seat. He was in no
hurry now. He had us where he wanted us and he knew it.

'This is real trouble,' I said. 'I don't like it one bit.'

'Don't talk to 'im any more than is necessary, you understand,' my companion said. 'Just sit tight and keep mum.'

Like an executioner approaching his victim, the policeman
came strolling slowly towards us. He was a big meaty man with
a belly, and his blue breeches were skintight around his enormous thighs. His goggles were pulled up on to the helmet,
showing a smouldering red face with wide cheeks.

We sat there like guilty schoolboys, waiting for him to arrive.

'Watch out for this man,' my passenger whispered. ' 'Ee looks
mean as the devil.'

The policeman came round to my open window and placed
one meaty hand on the sill. 'What's the hurry?' he said.

'No hurry, officer,' I answered.

'Perhaps there's a woman in the back having a baby and
you're rushing her to hospital? Is that it?'

'No, officer.'

'Or perhaps your house is on fire and you're dashing home to
rescue the family from upstairs?' His voice was dangerously
soft and mocking.

'My house isn't on fire, officer.'

'In that case,' he said, 'you've got yourself into a nasty mess,
haven't you? Do you know what the speed limit is in this
country?'

'Seventy,' I said.

'And do you mind telling me exactly what speed you were doing just now?'

I shrugged and didn't say anything.

When he spoke next, he raised his voice so loud that I jumped. *'One hundred and twenty miles per hour!'* he barked. 'That's *fifty* miles an hour over the limit!'

He turned his head and spat out a big gob of spit. It landed on the wing of my car and started sliding down over my beautiful blue paint. Then he turned back again and stared hard at my passenger. 'And who are you?' he asked sharply.

'He's a hitch-hiker,' I said. 'I'm giving him a lift.'

'I didn't ask you,' he said. 'I asked him.'

''Ave I done somethin' wrong?' my passenger asked. His voice was as soft and oily as haircream.

'That's more than likely,' the policeman answered. 'Anyway, you're a witness. I'll deal with you in a minute. Driving-licence,' he snapped, holding out his hand.

I gave him my driving-licence.

He unbuttoned the left-hand breast-pocket of his tunic and brought out the dreaded books of tickets. Carefully, he copied the name and address from my licence. Then he gave it back to me. He strolled round to the front of the car and read the number from the number-plate and wrote that down as well. He filled in the date, the time and the details of my offence. Then he tore out the top copy of the ticket. But before handing it to me, he checked that all the information had come through clearly on his own carbon copy. Finally, he replaced the book in his tunic pocket and fastened the button.

'Now you,' he said to my passenger, and he walked around to the other side of the car. From the other breast-pocket he produced a small black notebook. 'Name?' he snapped.

'Michael Fish,' my passenger said.

'Address?'

'Fourteen, Windsor Lane, Luton.'

'Show me something to prove this is your real name and address,' the policeman said.

My passenger fished in his pockets and came out with a driving-licence of his own. The policeman checked the name and address and handed it back to him. 'What's your job?' he asked sharply.

'I'm an 'od carrier.'

'A *what*?'

'An 'od carrier.'

'Spell it.'

'H-O-D C-A- . . .'

'That'll do. And what's a hod carrier, may I ask?'

'An 'od carrier, officer, is a person 'oo carries the cement up the ladder to the bricklayer. And the 'od is what 'ee carries it in. It's got a long 'andle, and on the top you've got two bits of wood set at an angle . . .'

'All right, all right. Who's your employer?'

'Don't 'ave one. I'm unemployed.'

The policeman wrote all this down in the black notebook. Then he returned the book to its pocket and did up the button.

'When I get back to the station I'm going to do a little checking up on you,' he said to my passenger.

'Me? What've I done wrong?' the rat-faced man asked.

'I don't like your face, that's all,' the policeman said. 'And we just might have a picture of it somewhere in our files.' He strolled round the car and returned to my window.

'I suppose you know you're in serious trouble,' he said to me.

'Yes, officer.'

'You won't be driving this fancy car of yours again for a very long time, not after *we've* finished with you. You won't be driving *any* car again come to that for several years. And a good thing, too. I hope they lock you up for a spell into the bargain.'

'You mean prison?' I asked, alarmed.

'Absolutely,' he said, smacking his lips. 'In the clink. Behind the bars. Along with all the other criminals who break the law. *And* a hefty fine into the bargain. Nobody will be more pleased about that than me. I'll see you in court, both of you. You'll be getting a summons to appear.'

He turned away and walked over to his motor-cycle. He flipped the prop stand back into position with his foot and swung his leg over the saddle. Then he kicked the starter and roared off up the road out of sight.

'Phew!' I gasped. 'That's done it.'

'We was caught,' my passenger said. 'We was caught good and proper.'

'I was caught, you mean.'

'That's right,' he said. 'What you goin' to do now, guv'nor?'

'I'm going straight up to London to talk to my solicitor,' I said. I started the car and drove on.

'You mustn't believe what 'ee said to you about goin' to prison,' my passenger said. 'They don't put nobody in the clink just for speedin'.'

'Are you sure of that?' I asked.

'I'm positive,' he answered. 'They can take your licence away and they can give you a whoppin' big fine, but that'll be the end of it.'

I felt tremendously relieved.

'By the way,' I said, 'why did you lie to him?'

'Who, me?' he said. 'What makes you think I lied?'

'You told him you were an unemployed hod carrier. But you told *me* you were in a highly skilled trade.'

'So I am,' he said. 'But it don't pay to tell everythin' to a copper.'

'So what *do* you do?' I asked him.

'Ah,' he said slyly. 'That'd be tellin', wouldn't it?'

'Is it something you're ashamed of?'

'Ashamed?' he cried. 'Me, ashamed of my job? I'm about as proud of it as anybody could be in the entire world!'

'Then why won't you tell me?'

'You writers really is nosey parkers, aren't you?' he said. 'And you ain't goin' to be 'appy, I don't think, until you've found out exactly what the answer is?'

'I don't really care one way or the other,' I told him, lying.

He gave me a crafty little ratty look out of the sides of his eyes. 'I think you do care,' he said. 'I can see it on your face that you think I'm in some kind of a very peculiar trade and you're just achin' to know what it is.'

I didn't like the way he read my thoughts. I kept quiet and stared at the road ahead.

'You'd be right, too,' he went on. 'I *am* in a very peculiar trade. I'm in the queerest peculiar trade of 'em all.'

I waited for him to go on.

'That's why I 'as to be extra careful 'oo I'm talkin' to, you see. 'Ow am I to know, for instance, you're not another copper in plain clothes?'

'Do I look like a copper?'

'No,' he said. 'You don't. And you ain't. Any fool could tell that.'

He took from his pocket a tin of tobacco and a packet of cigarette papers and started to roll a cigarette. I was watching him out of the corner of one eye, and the speed with which he performed this rather difficult operation was incredible. The cigarette was rolled and ready in about five seconds. He ran his tongue along the edge of the paper, stuck it down and popped the cigarette between his lips. Then, as if from nowhere, a lighter appeared in his hand. The lighter flamed. The cigarette was lit. The lighter disappeared. It was altogether a remarkable performance.

'I've never seen anyone roll a cigarette as fast as that,' I said.

'Ah,' he said, taking a deep suck of smoke. 'So you noticed.'

'Of course I noticed. It was quite fantastic.'

He sat back and smiled. It pleased him very much that I had noticed how quickly he could roll a cigarette. 'You want to know what makes me able to do it?' he asked.

'Go on then.'

'It's because I've got fantastic fingers. These fingers of mine,' he said, holding up both hands high in front of him, 'are quicker and cleverer than the fingers of the best piano player in the world!'

'Are you a piano player?'

'Don't be daft,' he said. 'Do I look like a piano player?'

I glanced at his fingers. They were so beautifully shaped, so slim and long and elegant, they didn't seem to belong to the rest of him at all. They looked more like the fingers of a brain surgeon or a watchmaker.

'My job,' he went on, 'is a hundred times more difficult than playin' the piano. Any twerp can learn to do that. There's titchy little kids learnin' to play the piano in almost any 'ouse you go into these days. That's right, ain't it?'

'More or less,' I said.

'Of course it's right. But there's not one person in ten million can learn to do what I do. Not one in ten million! 'Ow about that?'

'Amazing,' I said.

'You're darn right it's amazin',' he said.

'I think I know what you do,' I said. 'You do conjuring tricks. You're a conjurer.'

'Me?' he snorted. 'A conjurer? Can you picture me goin' round crummy kids' parties makin' rabbits come out of top 'ats?'

'Then you're a card player. You get people into card games and deal yourself marvellous hands.'

'Me! A rotten card-sharper!' he cried. 'That's a miserable racket if ever there was one.'

'All right. I give up.'

I was taking the car along slowly now, at no more than forty miles an hour, to make quite sure I wasn't stopped again. We had come on to the main London–Oxford road and were running down the hill towards Denham.

Suddenly, my passenger was holding up a black leather belt in his hand. 'Ever seen this before?' he asked. The belt had a brass buckle of unusual design.

'Hey!' I said. 'That's mine, isn't it? It *is* mine! Where did you get it?'

He grinned and waved the belt gently from side to side. 'Where d'you think I got it?' he said. 'Off the top of your trousers, of course.'

I reached down and felt for my belt. It was gone.

'You mean you took it off me while we've been driving along?' I asked, flabbergasted.

He nodded, watching me all the time with those little black ratty eyes.

'That's impossible,' I said. 'You'd have had to undo the buckle and slide the whole thing out through the loops all the way round. I'd have seen you doing it. And even if I hadn't seen you, I'd have felt it.'

'Ah, but you didn't, did you?' he said, triumphant. He dropped the belt on his lap, and now all at once there was a brown shoelace dangling from his fingers. 'And what about this, then?' he exclaimed, waving the shoelace.

'What about it?' I said.

'Anyone around 'ere missin' a shoelace?' he asked, grinning.

I glanced down at my shoes. The lace of one of them was missing. 'Good grief!' I said. 'How did you do that? I never saw you bending down.'

'You never saw nothin',' he said proudly. 'You never even saw me move an inch. And you know why?'

'Yes,' I said. 'Because you've got fantastic fingers.'

'Exactly right!' he cried. 'You catch on pretty quick, don't you?' He sat back and sucked away at his home-made cigarette, blowing the smoke out in a thin stream against the windshield. He knew he had impressed me greatly with those two tricks, and this made him very happy. 'I don't want to be late,' he said. 'What's time is it?'

'There's a clock in front of you,' I told him.

'I don't trust car clocks,' he said. 'What does your watch say?'

I hitched up my sleeve to look at the watch on my wrist. It wasn't there. I looked at the man. He looked back at me, grinning.

'You've taken that, too,' I said.

He held out his hand and there was my watch lying in his palm. 'Nice bit of stuff, this,' he said. 'Superior quality. Eighteen-carat gold. Easy to flog, too. It's never any trouble gettin' rid of quality goods.'

'I'd like it back, if you don't mind,' I said rather huffily.

He placed the watch carefully on the leather tray in front of him. 'I wouldn't nick anything from you, guv'nor,' he said. 'You're my pal. You're giving me a lift.'

'I'm glad to hear it,' I said.

'All I'm doin' is answerin' your questions,' he went on. 'You asked me what I did for a livin' and I'm showin' you.'

'What else have you got of mine?'

He smiled again, and now he started to take from the pocket of his jacket one thing after another that belonged to me – my driving-licence, a key-ring with four keys on it, some pound notes, a few coins, a letter from my publishers, my diary, a stubby old pencil, a cigarette-lighter, and last of all, a beautiful old sapphire ring with pearls around it belonging to my wife. I was taking the ring up to the jeweller in London because one of the pearls was missing.

'Now *there's* another lovely piece of goods,' he said, turning the ring over in his fingers. 'That's eighteenth century, if I'm not mistaken, from the reign of King George the Third.'

'You're right,' I said, impressed. 'You're absolutely right.'

He put the ring on the leather tray with the other items.

'So you're a pickpocket,' I said.

'I don't like that word,' he answered. 'It's a coarse and vulgar word. Pickpockets is coarse and vulgar people who only do easy little amateur jobs. They lift money from blind old ladies.'

'What do you call yourself, then?'

'Me? I'm a fingersmith. I'm a professional fingersmith.' He spoke the words solemnly and proudly, as though he were telling me he was the President of the Royal College of Surgeons or the Archbishop of Canterbury.

'I've never heard that word before,' I said. 'Did you invent it?'

'Of course I didn't invent it,' he replied. 'It's the name given to them who's risen to the very top of the profession. You've 'eard of a goldsmith and a silversmith, for instance. They're experts with gold and silver. I'm an expert with my fingers, so I'm a fingersmith.'

'It must be an interesting job.'

'It's a marvellous job,' he answered. 'It's lovely.'

'And that's why you go to the races?'

'Race meetings is easy meat,' he said. 'You just stand around after the race, watchin' for the lucky ones to queue up and draw their money. And when you see someone collectin' a big bundle of notes, you simply follows after 'im and 'elps yourself. But don't get me wrong, guv'nor. I never takes nothin' from a loser. Nor from poor people neither. I only go after them as can afford it, the winners and the rich.'

'That's very thoughtful of you,' I said. 'How often do you get caught?'

'Caught?' he cried, disgusted. '*Me* get caught! It's only pickpockets get caught. Fingersmiths never. Listen, I could take the false teeth out of your mouth if I wanted to and you wouldn't even catch me!'

'I don't have false teeth,' I said.

'I know you don't,' he answered. 'Otherwise I'd 'ave 'ad 'em out long ago!'

I believed him. Those long slim fingers of his seemed able to do anything.

We drove on for a while without talking.

'That policeman's going to check up on you pretty thoroughly,' I said. 'Doesn't that worry you a bit?'

'Nobody's checkin' up on me,' he said.

'Of course they are. He's got your name and address written down most carefully in his black book.'

The man gave me another of his sly, ratty little smiles. 'Ah,' he said. 'So 'ee 'as. But I'll bet 'ee ain't got it all written down in 'is memory as well. I've never known a copper yet with a decent memory. Some of 'em can't even remember their own names.'

'What's memory got to do with it?' I asked. 'It's written down in his book, isn't it?'

'Yes, guv'nor, it is. But the trouble is, 'ee's lost the book. 'Ee's lost both books, the one with my name in it *and* the one with yours.'

In the long delicate fingers of his right hand, the man was holding up in triumph the two books he had taken from the policeman's pockets. 'Easiest job I ever done,' he announced proudly.

I nearly swerved the car into a milk-truck, I was so excited.

'That copper's got nothin' on either of us now,' he said.

'You're a genius!' I cried.

''Ee's got no names, no addresses, no car number, no nothin',' he said.

'You're brilliant!'

'I think you'd better pull in off this main road as soon as possible,' he said. 'Then we'd better build a little bonfire and burn these books.'

'You're a fantastic fellow,' I exclaimed.

'Thank you, guv'nor,' he said. 'It's always nice to be appreciated.'

# The Umbrella Man

I'm going to tell you about a funny thing that happened to my mother and me yesterday evening. I am twelve years old and I'm a girl. My mother is thirty-four but I am nearly as tall as her already.

Yesterday afternoon, my mother took me up to London to see the dentist. He found one hole. It was in a back tooth and he filled it without hurting me too much. After that, we went to a café. I had a banana split and my mother had a cup of coffee. By the time we got up to leave, it was about six o'clock.

When we came out of the café it had started to rain. 'We must get a taxi,' my mother said. We were wearing ordinary hats and coats, and it was raining quite hard.

'Why don't we go back into the café and wait for it to stop?' I said. I wanted another of those banana splits. They were gorgeous.

'It isn't going to stop,' my mother said. 'We must get home.'

We stood on the pavement in the rain, looking for a taxi. Lots of them came by but they all had passengers inside them. 'I wish we had a car with a chauffeur,' my mother said.

Just then, a man came up to us. He was a small man and he was pretty old, probably seventy or more. He raised his hat politely and said to my mother, 'Excuse me. I do hope you will excuse me ...' He had a fine white moustache and bushy white eyebrows and a wrinkly pink face. He was sheltering under an umbrella which he held high over his head.

'Yes?' my mother said, very cool and distant.

'I wonder if I could ask a small favour of you,' he said. 'It is only a very small favour.'

I saw my mother looking at him suspiciously. She is a suspicious person, my mother. She is especially suspicious of two things – strange men and boiled eggs. When she cuts the top off a boiled egg, she pokes around inside it with her spoon as though expecting to find a mouse or something. With strange men, she has a golden rule which says, 'The nicer the man seems to be, the more suspicious you must become.' This little old man was particularly nice. He was polite. He was well-spoken. He was well-dressed. He was a real gentleman. The reason I knew he was a gentleman was because of his shoes. 'You can always spot a gentleman by the shoes he wears,' was another of my mother's favourite sayings. This man had beautiful brown shoes.

'The truth of the matter is,' the little man was saying, 'I've got myself into a bit of a scrape. I need some help. Not much, I assure you. It's almost nothing, in fact, but I do need it. You see, madam, old people like me often become terribly forgetful ...'

My mother's chin was up and she was staring down at him along the full length of her nose. It is a fearsome thing, this frosty-nosed stare of my mother's. Most people go to pieces completely when she gives it to them. I once saw my own headmistress begin to stammer and simper like an idiot when my mother gave her a really foul frosty-noser. But the little man on the pavement with the umbrella over his head didn't bat an eyelid. He gave a gentle smile and said, 'I beg you to believe, madam, that I am not in the habit of stopping ladies in the street and telling them my troubles.'

'I should hope not,' my mother said.

I felt quite embarrassed by my mother's sharpness. I wanted to say to her, 'Oh, mummy, for heaven's sake, he's a very very old man, and he's sweet and polite, and he's in some sort of trouble, so don't be so beastly to him.' But I didn't say anything.

The little man shifted his umbrella from one hand to the other. 'I've never forgotten it before,' he said.

'You've never forgotten what?' my mother asked sternly.

'My wallet,' he said. 'I must have left it in my other jacket. Isn't that the silliest thing to do?'

'Are you asking me to give you money?' my mother said.

'Oh, good gracious me, no!' he cried. 'Heaven forbid I should ever do that!'

'Then what *are* you asking?' my mother said. 'Do hurry up. We're getting soaked to the skin standing here.'

'I know you are,' he said. 'And that is why I'm offering you this umbrella of mine to protect you, and to keep forever, if ... if only ...'

'If only what?' my mother said.

'If only you would give me in return a pound for my taxi-fare just to get me home.'

My mother was still suspicious. 'If you had no money in the first place,' she said, 'then how did you get here?'

'I walked,' he answered. 'Every day I go for a lovely long walk and then I summon a taxi to take me home. I do it every day of the year.'

'Why don't you walk home now?' my mother asked.

'Oh, I wish I could,' he said. 'I do wish I could. But I don't think I could manage it on these silly old legs of mine. I've gone too far already.'

My mother stood there chewing her lower lip. She was beginning to melt a bit, I could see that. And the idea of getting an umbrella to shelter under must have tempted her a good deal.

'It's a lovely umbrella,' the little man said.

'So I've noticed,' my mother said.

'It's silk,' he said.

'I can see that.'

'Then why don't you take it, madam,' he said. 'It cost me over twenty pounds, I promise you. But that's of no importance so long as I can get home and rest these old legs of mine.'

I saw my mother's hand feeling for the clasp on her purse. She saw me watching her. I was giving her one of my *own* frosty-nosed looks this time and she knew exactly what I was telling her. Now listen, mummy, I was telling her, you simply *mustn't* take advantage of a tired old man in this way. It's a rotten thing to do. My mother paused and looked back at me. Then she said to the little man, 'I don't think it's quite right that I should take a silk umbrella from you worth twenty pounds. I think I'd just better *give* you the taxi-fare and be done with it.'

'No, no, no!' he cried. 'It's out of the question! I wouldn't dream of it! Not in a million years! I would never accept money from you like that! Take the umbrella, dear lady, and keep the rain off your shoulders!'

My mother gave me a triumphant sideways look. There you are, she was telling me. You're wrong. He *wants* me to have it.

She fished into her purse and took out a pound note. She held it out to the little man. He took it and handed her the umbrella. He pocketed the pound, raised his hat, gave a quick bow from the waist, and said, 'Thank you, madam, thank you.' Then he was gone.

'Come under here and keep dry, darling,' my mother said. 'Aren't we lucky. I've never had a silk umbrella before. I couldn't afford it.'

'Why were you so horrid to him in the beginning?' I asked.

'I wanted to satisfy myself he wasn't a trickster,' she said. 'And I did. He was a gentleman. I'm very pleased I was able to help him.'

'Yes, mummy,' I said.

'A *real* gentleman,' she went on. 'Wealthy, too, otherwise he wouldn't have had a silk umbrella. I shouldn't be surprised if he isn't a titled person. Sir Harry Goldsworthy or something like that.'

'Yes, mummy.'

'This will be a good lesson to you,' she went on. 'Never rush things. Always take your time when you are summing someone up. Then you'll never make mistakes.'

'There he goes,' I said. 'Look.'

'Where?'

'Over there. He's crossing the street. Goodness, mummy, what a hurry he's in.'

We watched the little man as he dodged nimbly in and out of the traffic. When he reached the other side of the street, he turned left, walking very fast.

'He doesn't look very tired to me, does he to you, mummy?'

My mother didn't answer.

'He doesn't look as though he's trying to get a taxi, either,' I said.

79

My mother was standing very still and stiff, staring across the street at the little man. We could see him clearly. He was in a terrific hurry. He was bustling along the pavement, sidestepping the other pedestrians and swinging his arms like a soldier on the march.

'He's up to something,' my mother said, stony-faced.

'But what?'

'I don't know,' my mother snapped. 'But I'm going to find out. Come with me.' She took my arm and we crossed the street together. Then we turned left.

'Can you see him?' my mother asked.

'Yes. There he is. He's turning right down the next street.'

We came to the corner and turned right. The little man was about twenty yards ahead of us. He was scuttling along like a rabbit and we had to walk fast to keep up with him. The rain was pelting down harder than ever now and I could see it dripping from the brim of his hat on to his shoulders. But we were snug and dry under our lovely big silk umbrella.

'What *is* he up to?' my mother said.

'What if he turns round and sees us?' I asked.

'I don't care if he does,' my mother said. 'He lied to us. He said he was too tired to walk any further and he's practically running us off our feet! He's a barefaced liar! He's a crook!'

'You mean he's *not* a titled gentleman?' I asked.

'Be quiet,' she said.

At the next crossing, the little man turned right again.

Then he turned left.

Then right.

'I'm not giving up now,' my mother said.

'He's disappeared!' I cried. 'Where's he gone?'

'He went in that door!' my mother said. 'I saw him! Into that house! Great heavens, it's a pub!'

It was a pub. In big letters right across the front it said THE RED LION.

'You're not going in, are you, mummy?'

'No,' she said. 'We'll watch from outside.'

There was a big plate-glass window along the front of the pub, and although it was a bit steamy on the inside, we could see through it very well if we went close.

We stood huddled together outside the pub window. I was clutching my mother's arm. The big raindrops were making a loud noise on our umbrella. 'There he is,' I said. 'Over there.'

The room we were looking into was full of people and cigarette smoke, and our little man was in the middle of it all. He was now without his hat or coat, and he was edging his way through the crowd towards the bar. When he reached it, he placed both hands on the bar itself and spoke to the barman. I saw his lips moving as he gave his order. The barman turned away from him for a few seconds and came back with a smallish tumbler filled to the brim with light brown liquid. The little man placed a pound note on the counter.

'That's my pound!' my mother hissed. 'By golly, he's got a nerve!'

'What's in the glass?' I asked.

'Whisky,' my mother said. 'Neat whisky.'

The barman didn't give him any change from the pound.

'That must be a treble whisky,' my mother said.

'What's a treble?' I asked.

'Three times the normal measure,' she answered.

The little man picked up the glass and put it to his lips. He tilted it gently. Then he tilted it higher ... and higher ... and higher ... and very soon all the whisky had disappeared down his throat in one long pour.

'That was a jolly expensive drink,' I said.

'It's ridiculous!' my mother said. 'Fancy paying a pound for something you swallow in one go!'

'It cost him more than a pound,' I said. 'It cost him a twenty-pound silk umbrella.'

'So it did,' my mother said. 'He must be mad.'

The little man was standing by the bar with the empty glass in his hand. He was smiling now, and a sort of golden glow of pleasure was spreading over his round pink face. I saw his tongue come out to lick the white moustache, as though searching for the last drop of that precious whisky.

Slowly, he turned away from the bar and edged back through the crowd to where his hat and coat were hanging. He put on his hat. He put on his coat. Then, in a manner so superbly cool and casual that you hardly noticed anything at all, he lifted from the coat-rack one of the many wet umbrellas hanging there, and off he went.

'Did you see that!' my mother shrieked. 'Did you see what he did!'

'Ssshh!' I whispered. 'He's coming out!'

We lowered the umbrella to hide our faces, and peeped out from under it.

Out he came. But he never looked in our direction. He opened his new umbrella over his head and scurried off down the road the way he had come.

'So that's his little game!' my mother said.

'Neat,' I said. 'Super.'

We followed him back to the main street where we had first met him, and we watched him as he proceeded, with no trouble at all, to exchange his new umbrella for another pound note. This time it was with a tall thin fellow who didn't even have a coat or hat. And as soon as the transaction was completed, our little man trotted off down the street and was lost in the crowd. But this time he went in the opposite direction.

'You see how clever he is!' my mother said. 'He never goes to the same pub twice!'

'He could go on doing this all night,' I said.

'Yes,' my mother said. 'Of course. But I'll bet he prays like mad for rainy days.'

# Mr Botibol

Mr Botibol pushed his way through the revolving doors and emerged into the large foyer of the hotel. He took off his hat, and holding it in front of him with both hands, he advanced nervously a few paces, paused and stood looking around him, searching the faces of the lunchtime crowd. Several people turned and stared at him in mild astonishment, and he heard – or he thought he heard – at least one woman's voice saying, 'My dear, *do* look what's just come in!'

At last he spotted Mr Clements sitting at a small table in the far corner, and he hurried over to him. Clements had seen him coming, and now, as he watched Mr Botibol threading his way cautiously between the tables and the people, walking on his toes in such a meek and self-effacing manner and clutching his hat before him with both hands, he thought how wretched it must be for any man to look as conspicuous and as odd as this Botibol. He resembled, to an extraordinary degree, an asparagus. His long narrow stalk did not appear to have any shoulders at all; it merely tapered upwards, growing gradually narrower and narrower until it came to a kind of point at the top of the small bald head. He was tightly encased in a shiny blue double-breasted suit, and this, for some curious reason, accentuated the illusion of a vegetable to a preposterous degree.

Clements stood up, they shook hands, and then at once, even before they had sat down again, Mr Botibol said, 'I have decided, yes I have decided to accept the offer which you made to me before you left my office last night.'

For some days Clements had been negotiating, on behalf of clients, for the purchase of the firm known as Botibol & Co., of which Mr Botibol was sole owner, and the night before, Clements had made his first offer. This was merely an exploratory, much-too-low bid, a kind of signal to the seller that the buyers were seriously interested. And by God, thought

Clements, the poor fool has gone and accepted it. He nodded gravely many times in an effort to hide his astonishment, and he said, 'Good, good. I'm so glad to hear that, Mr Botibol.' Then he signalled a waiter and said, 'Two large martinis.'

'No, please!' Mr Botibol lifted both hands in horrified protest.

'Come on,' Clements said. 'This is an occasion.'

'I drink very little, and never, no never during the middle of the day.'·

But Clements was in a gay mood now and he took no notice. He ordered the martinis and when they came along Mr Botibol was forced, by the banter and good-humour of the other, to drink to the deal which had just been concluded. Clements then spoke briefly about the drawing up and signing of documents, and when all that had been arranged, he called for two more cocktails. Again Mr Botibol protested, but not quite so vigorously this time, and Clements ordered the drinks and then he turned and smiled at the other man in a friendly way. 'Well, Mr Botibol,' he said, 'now that it's all over, I suggest we have a pleasant non-business lunch together. What d'you say to that? And it's on me.'

'As you wish, as you wish,' Mr Botibol answered without any enthusiasm. He had a small melancholy voice and a way of pronouncing each word separately and slowly, as though he was explaining something to a child.

When they went into the dining-rom Clements ordered a bottle of Lafite 1912 and a couple of plump roast partridges to go with it. He had already calculated in his head the amount of his commission and he was feeling fine. He began to make bright conversation, switching smoothly from one subject to another in the hope of touching on something that might interest his guest. But it was no good. Mr Botibol appeared to be only half listening. Every now and then he inclined his small bald head a little to one side or the other and said, 'Indeed.' When the wine came along Clements tried to have a talk about that.

'I am sure it is excellent,' Mr Botibol said, 'but please give me only a drop.'

Clements told a funny story. When it was over, Mr Botibol

regarded him solemnly for a few moments, then he said, 'How amusing.' After that Clements kept his mouth shut and they ate in silence. Mr Botibol was drinking his wine and he didn't seem to object when his host reached over and refilled his glass. By the time they had finished eating, Clements estimated privately that his guest had consumed at least three-quarters of the bottle.

'A cigar, Mr Botibol?'

'Oh no, thank you.'

'A little brandy?'

'No really, I am not accustomed ...' Clements noticed that the man's cheeks were slightly flushed and that his eyes had become bright and watery. Might as well get the old boy properly drunk while I'm about it, he thought, and to the waiter he said, 'Two brandies.'

When the brandies arrived, Mr Botibol looked at his large glass suspiciously for a while, then he picked it up, took one quick birdlike sip and put it down again. 'Mr Clements,' he said suddenly, 'how I envy you.'

'Me? But why?'

'I will tell you, Mr Clements, I will tell you, if I may make so bold.' There was a nervous, mouselike quality in his voice which made it seem he was apologizing for everything he said.

'Please tell me,' Clements said.

'It is because to me you appear to have made such a success of your life.'

He's going to get melancholy drunk, Clements thought. He's one of the ones that gets melancholy and I can't stand it. 'Success,' he said, 'I don't see anything especially successful about me.'

'Oh yes, indeed. Your whole life, if I may say so,, Mr Clements, appears to be such a pleasant and successful thing.'

'I'm a very ordinary person,' Clements said. He was trying to figure just how drunk the other really was.

'I believe,' said Mr Botibol, speaking slowly, separating each word carefully from the other, 'I believe that the wine has gone a little to my head, but ...' He paused, searching for words. '... But I do want to ask you just one question.' He had poured some salt on to the tablecloth and he was shaping it into a little mountain with the tip of one finger.

'Mr Clements,' he said without looking up, 'do you think that it is possible for a man to live to the age of fifty-two without ever during his whole life having experienced one single small success in anything that he has done?'

'My dear Mr Botibol,' Clements laughed, 'everyone has his little successes from time to time, however small they may be.'

'Oh no,' Mr Botibol said gently. 'You are wrong. I, for example, cannot remember having had a single success of any sort during my whole life.'

'Now come!' Clements said, smiling, 'That can't be true. Why only this morning you sold your business for a hundred thousand. I call that one hell of a success.'

'The business was left me by my father. When he died nine years ago, it was worth four times as much. Under my direction it has lost three-quarters of its value. You can hardly call that a success.'

Clements knew this was true. 'Yes yes, all right,' he said. 'That may be so, but all the same you know as well as I do that every man alive has his quota of little successes. Not big ones maybe. But lots of little ones. I mean, after all, goddammit, even scoring goal at school was a little success, a little triumph, at the time; or making some runs or learning to swim. One forgets about them, that's all. One just forgets.'

'I never scored a goal,' Mr Botibol said. 'And I never learned to swim.'

Clements threw up his hands and made exasperated noises. 'Yes yes, I know, but don't you see, don't you see there are thousands, literally thousands of other things, things like ... well ... like catching a good fish, or fixing the motor of the car, or pleasing someone with a present, or growing a decent row of French beans, or winning a little bet or ... or ... why hell, one can go on listing them for ever!'

'Perhaps *you* can, Mr Clements, but to the best of my knowledge, I have never done any of those things. That is what I am trying to tell you.'

Clements put down his brandy glass and stared with new interest at the remarkable shoulderless person who sat facing him. He was annoyed and he didn't feel in the least sympathetic. The man didn't inspire sympathy. He was a fool. He must be a fool. A tremendous and absolute fool. Clements had a sudden desire to embarrass the man as much as he could. 'What about women, Mr Botibol?' There was no apology for the question in the tone of his voice.

'Women?'

'Yes women! Every man under the sun, even the most wretched filthy down-and-out tramp has some time or other had some sort of silly little success with ...'

'Never!' cried Mr Botibol with sudden vigour. 'No sir, never!'

I'm going to hit him, Clements told himself. I can't stand this any longer and if I'm not careful I'm going to jump right up and hit him. 'You mean you don't like them?' he said.

'Oh dear me yes, of course I like them. As a matter of fact I admire them very much, very much indeed. But I'm afraid ... oh dear me ... I do not know quite how to say it ... I am afraid that I do not seem to get along with them very well. I never have. Never. You see, Mr Clements, I *look* so queer. I know I do. They stare at me, and often I see them laughing at me. I have never been able to get within ... well, within striking distance of them, as you might say.' The trace of a smile, weak and infinitely sad, flickered around the corners of his mouth.

Clements had had enough. He mumbled something about how he was sure Mr Botibol was exaggerating the situation, then he glanced at his watch, called for the bill, and said he was sorry but he would have to get back to the office.

They parted in the street outside the hotel and Mr Botibol took a cab back to his house. He opened the front door, went into the living-room and switched on the radio; then he sat down in a large leather chair, leaned back and closed his eyes. He didn't feel exactly giddy, but there was a singing in his ears and his thoughts were coming and going more quickly than usual. That solicitor gave me too much wine, he told himself. I'll stay here for a while and listen to some music and I expect I'll go to sleep and after that I'll feel better.

They were playing a symphony on the radio. Mr Botibol had always been a casual listener to symphony concerts and he knew enough to identify this as one of Beethoven's. But now, as he lay back in his chair listening to the marvellous music, a new thought began to expand slowly within his tipsy mind. It wasn't a dream because he was not asleep. It was a clear conscious thought and it was this: I am the composer of this music. I am a great composer. This is my latest symphony and this is the first performance. The huge hall is packed with people – critics, musicians and music-lovers from all over the country – and I am up there in front of the orchestra, conducting.

Mr Botibol could see the whole thing. He could see himself up on the rostrum dressed in a white tie and tails, and before him was the orchestra, the massed violins on his left, the violas in front, the cellos on his right, and back of them were all the woodwinds and bassoons and drums and cymbals, the players watching every movement of his baton with an intense, almost a fanatical reverence. Behind him, in the half-darkness of the huge hall, was row upon row of white enraptured faces, looking up towards him, listening with growing excitement as yet another new symphony by the greatest composer the world had ever seen unfolded itself majestically before them. Some of the audience were clenching their fists and digging their nails into the palms of their hands because the music was so beautiful that they could hardly stand it. Mr Botibol became so carried away by this exciting vision that he began to swing his arms in time with the music in the manner of a conductor. He found it was such fun doing this that he decided to stand up, facing the radio, in order to give himself more freedom of movement.

He stood there in the middle of the room, tall, thin and shoulderless, dressed in his tight blue double-breasted suit, his small bald head jerking from side to side as he waved his arms in the air. He knew the symphony well enuogh to be able occasionally to anticipate changes in tempo or volume, and when the music became loud and fast he beat the air so vigorously that he nearly knocked himself over; when it was soft and hushed, he leaned forward to quieten the players with gentle movements of his outstretched hands; and all the time he could feel the presence of the huge audience behind him, tense, immobile, listening. When at last the symphony swelled to its tremendous conclusion, Mr Botibol became more frenzied than ever and his face seemed to thrust itself round to one side in an agony of effort as he tried to force more and still more power from his orchestra during those final mighty chords.

Then it was over. The announcer was saying something, but Mr Botibol quickly switched off the radio and collapsed into his chair, blowing heavily.

'Phew!' he said aloud. 'My goodness gracious me, what *have* I been doing!' Small globules of sweat were oozing out all over his face and forehead, trickling down his neck inside his collar. He pulled out a handkerchief and wiped them away, and he lay there for a while, panting, exhausted, but exceedingly exhilarated.

'Well, I must say,' he gasped, still speaking aloud, 'that *was* fun. I don't know that I have ever had such fun before in all my life. My goodness, it *was* fun, it really *was*!' Almost at once he began to play with the idea of doing it again. But should he? Should he allow himself to do it again? There was no denying that now, in retrospect, he felt a little guilty about the whole business, and soon he began to wonder whether there wasn't something downright immoral about it all. Letting himself go like that! And imagining he was a genius! It was wrong. He was sure other people didn't do it. And what if Mason had come in in the middle and seen him at it! That would have been terrible!

He reached for the paper and pretended to read it, but soon he was searching furtively among the radio programmes for the evening. He put his finger under a line which said '8·30 Symphony Concert. Brahms Symphony No. 2'. He stared at it for a long time. The letters in the word 'Brahms' began to blur and recede, and gradually they disappeared altogether and were replaced by letters which spelt 'Botibol'. Botibol's Symphony No. 2. It was printed quite clearly. He was reading it now, this moment. 'Yes, yes,' he whispered. 'First performance. The world is waiting to hear it. Will it be as great, they are asking, will it perhaps be greater than his earlier work? And the composer himself has been persuaded to conduct. He is shy and retiring, hardly ever appears in public, but on this occasion he has been persuaded ...'

Mr Botibol leaned forward in his chair and pressed the bell

beside the fireplace. Mason, the butler, the only other person in the house, ancient, small and grave, appeared at the door.

'Er ... Mason, have we any wine in the house?'

'Wine, sir?'

'Yes, wine.'

'Oh no, sir. We haven't had any wine this fifteen or sixteen years. Your father, sir ...'

'I know, Mason, I know, but will you get some please. I want a bottle with my dinner.'

The butler was shaken. 'Very well, sir, and what shall it be?'

'Claret, Mason. The best you can obtain. Get a case. Tell them to send it round at once.'

When he was alone again, he was momentarily appalled by the simple manner in which he had made this decision. Wine for dinner! Just like that! Well, yes, why not? Why ever not now he came to think of it? He was his own master. And anyway it was essential that he have wine. It seemed to have a good effect, a very good effect indeed. He wanted it and he was going to have it and to hell with Mason.

He rested for the remainder of the afternoon, and at seven-thirty Mason announced dinner. The bottle of wine was on the table and he began to drink it. He didn't give a damn about the way Mason watched him as he refilled his glass. Three times he refilled it; then he left the table saying that he was not to be disturbed and returned to the living-room. There was quarter of an hour to wait. He could think of nothing now except the coming concert. He lay back in the chair and allowed his thoughts to wander deliciously towards eight-thirty. He was the great composer waiting impatiently in his dressing-room in the concert-hall. He could hear in the distance the murmur of excitement from the crowd as they settled themselves in their seats. He knew what they were saying to each other. Same sort of thing the newspapers had been saying for months; Botibol is a genius; greater, far greater than Beethoven or Bach or Brahms or Mozart or any of them. Each new work of his is more magnificent than the last. What will the next one be like? We can hardly wait to hear it! Oh yes, he knew what they were saying. He stood up and began to pace the room. It was nearly time now. He seized a pencil from the table to use as a baton, then he switched on the radio. The announcer had just finished the preliminaries and suddenly there was a burst of applause which meant that the conductor was coming on to the platform. The previous concert in the afternoon had been from gramophone records, but this one was the real thing. Mr Botibol turned around, faced the fireplace and bowed graciously from the waist. Then he turned back to the radio and lifted his baton. The clapping stopped. There was a moment's silence. Someone in the audience coughed. Mr Botibol waited. The symphony began.

Once again, as he began to conduct, he could see clearly before him the whole orchestra and the faces of the players and even the expressions on their faces. Three of the violinists had grey hair. One of the cellists was very fat, another wore heavy brown-rimmed glasses, and there was a man in the second row playing a horn who had a twitch on one side of his face. But they were all magnificent. And so was the music. During certain impressive passages Mr Botibol experienced a feeling of exultation so powerful that it made him cry out for joy, and once during the Third Movement, a little shiver of ecstasy radiated spontaneously from his solar plexus and moved downward over the skin of his stomach like needles. But the thunderous applause and the cheering which came at the end of the symphony was the most splendid thing of all. He turned slowly towards the fireplace and bowed. The clapping continued and he went on bowing until at last the noise died away and the announcer's voice jerked him suddenly back into the living-room. He switched off the radio and collapsed into his chair, exhausted but very happy.

As he lay there, smiling with pleasure, wiping his wet face, panting for breath, he was already making plans for his next performance. But why not do it properly? Why not convert one of the rooms into a sort of concert-hall and have a stage and rows of chairs and do the thing properly? And have a gramophone so that one could perform at any time without having to rely on the radio programme. Yes by heavens, he would do it!

The next morning Mr Botibol arranged with a firm of decorators that the largest room in the house be converted into a

miniature concert-hall. There was to be a raised stage at one
end and the rest of the floor-space was to be filled with rows of
red plush seats. 'I'm going to have some little concerts here,' he
told the man from the firm, and the man nodded and said that
would be very nice. At the same time he ordered a radio shop
to instal an expensive self-changing gramophone with two
powerful amplifiers, one on the stage, the other at the back of
the auditorium. When he had done this, he went off and bought
all of Beethoven's nine symphonies on gramophone records;
and from a place which specialized in recorded sound effects
he ordered several records of clapping and applauding by enthusiastic audiences. Finally he bought himself a conductor's
baton, a slim ivory stick which lay in a case lined with blue
silk.

In eight days the room was ready. Everything was perfect:
the red chairs, the aisle down the centre and even a little dais
on the platform with a brass rail running round it for the conductor. Mr Botibol decided to give the first concert that evening after dinner.

At seven o'clock he went up to his bedroom and changed
into white tie and tails. He felt marvellous. When he looked at
himself in the mirror, the sight of his own grotesque shoulderless figure didn't worry him in the least. A great composer, he
thought, smiling, can look as he damn well pleases. People
*expect* him to look peculiar. All the same he wished he had
some hair on his head. He would have liked to let it grow
rather long. He went downstairs to dinner, ate his food rapidly,
drank half a bottle of wine and felt better still. 'Don't worry
about me, Mason,' he said. 'I'm not mad. I'm just enjoying
myself.'

'Yes, sir.'

'I shan't want you any more. Please see that I'm not disturbed.' Mr Botibol went from the dining-room into the miniature concert-hall. He took out the records of Beethoven's First
Symphony, but before putting them on the gramophone, he
place two other records with them. The one, which was to be
played first of all, before the music began, was labelled 'pro-
longed enthusiastic applause'. The other, which would come at
the end of the symphony, was labelled 'Sustained applause,

clapping, cheering, shouts of encore'. By a simple mechanical device on the record changer, the gramophone people had arranged that the sound from the first and the last records – the applause – would come only from the loudspeaker in the auditorium. The sound from all the others – the music – would come from the speaker hidden among the chairs of the orchestra. When he had arranged the records in the correct order, he placed them on the machine but he didn't switch on at once. Instead he turned out all the lights in the room except one small one which lit up the conductor's dais and he sat down in a chair up on the stage, closed his eyes and allowed his thoughts to wander into the usual delicious regions: the great composer, nervous, impatient, waiting to present his latest masterpiece, the audience assembling, the murmur of their excited talk, and so on. Having dreamed himself right into the part, he stood up, picked up his baton and switched on the gramophone.

A tremendous wave of clapping filled the room. Mr Botibol walked across the stage, mounted the dais, faced the audience and bowed. In the darkness he could just make out the faint outline of the seats on either side of the centre aisle, but he couldn't see the faces of the people. They were making enough noise. What an ovation! Mr Botibol turned and faced the orchestra. The applause behind him died down. The next record dropped. The symphony began.

This time it was more thrilling than ever, and during the performance he registered any number of prickly sensations around his solar plexus. Once, when it suddenly occurred to him that this music was being broadcast all over the world, a sort of shiver ran right down the length of his spine. But by far the most exciting part was the applause which came at the end. They cheered and clapped and stamped and shouted encore! encore! encore! and he turned towards the darkened auditorium and bowed gravely to the left and right. Then he went off the stage, but they called him back. He bowed several more times and went off again, and again they called him back. The audience had gone mad. They simply wouldn't let him go. It was terrific. It was truly a terrific ovation.

Later, when he was resting in his chair in the other room, he was still enjoying it. He closed his eyes because he didn't want anything to break the spell. He lay there and he felt like he was floating. It was really a most marvellous floating feeling, and when he went upstairs and undressed and got into bed, it was still with him.

The following evening he conducted Beethoven's – or rather Botibol's – Second Symphony, and they were just as mad about that one as the first. The next few nights he played one symphony a night, and at the end of nine evenings he had worked through all nine of Beethoven's symphonies. It got more exciting every time because before each concert the audience kept saying 'He can't do it again, not another masterpiece. It's not humanly possible.' But he did. They were all of them equally magnificent. The last symphony, the Ninth, was especially exciting because here the composer surprised and delighted everyone by suddenly providing a choral masterpiece. He had to conduct a huge choir as well as the orchestra itself, and Benjamino Gigli had flown over from Italy to take the tenor part. Enrico Pinza sang bass. At the end of it the audience shouted themselves hoarse. The whole musical world was on its feet cheering, and on all sides they were saying how you never could tell what wonderful things to expect next from this amazing person.

The composing, presenting and conducting of nine great symphonies in as many days is a fair achievement for any man, and it was not astonishing that it went a little to Mr Botibol's head. He decided now that he would once again surprise his public. He would compose a mass of marvellous piano music and he himself would give the recitals. So early the next morning he set out for the showroom of the people who sold Bechsteins and Steinways. He felt so brisk and fit that he walked all the way, and as he walked he hummed little snatches of new and lovely tunes for the piano. His head was full of them. All the time they kept coming to him and once, suddenly, he had the feeling that thousands of small notes, some white, some black, were cascading down a shute into his head through a hole in his head, and that his brain, his amazing musical brain, was receiving them as fast as they could come and unscrambling them and arranging them neatly in a certain order so that they made wondrous melodies. There were Nocturnes, there were Études and there were Waltzes, and soon, he told himself, soon he would give them all to a grateful and admiring world.

When he arrived at the piano-shop, he pushed the door open and walked in with an air almost of confidence. He had changed much in the last few days. Some of his nervousness had left him and he was no longer wholly preoccupied with what others thought of his appearance. 'I want,' he said to the salesman, 'a concert grand, but you must arrange it so that when the notes are struck, no sound is produced.'

The salesman leaned forward and raised his eyebrows.

'Could that be arranged?' Mr Botibol asked.

'Yes, sir, I think so, if you desire it. But might I inquire what you intend to use the instrument for?'

'If you want to know, I'm going to pretend I'm Chopin. I'm going to sit and play while a gramophone makes the music. It gives me a kick.' It came out, just like that, and Mr Botibol didn't know what had made him say it. But it was done now and he had said it and that was that. In a way he felt relieved, because he had proved he didn't mind telling people what he was doing. The man would probably answer what a jolly good idea. Or he might not. He might say well you ought to be locked up.

'So now you know,' Mr Botibol said.

The salesman laughed out loud. 'Ha ha! Ha ha ha! That's very good, sir. Very good indeed. Serves me right for asking silly questions.' He stopped suddenly in the middle of the laugh and looked hard at Mr Botibol. 'Of course, sir, you probably know that we sell a simple noiseless keyboard specially for silent practising.'

'I want a concert grand,' Mr Botibol said. The salesman looked at him again.

Mr Botibol chose his piano and got out of the shop as quickly as possible. He went on to the store that sold gramophone records and there he ordered a quantity of albums containing recordings of all Chopin's Nocturnes, Études and Waltzes, played by Arthur Rubinstein.

'My goodness, you *are* going to have a lovely time!'

Mr Botibol turned and saw standing beside him at the counter a squat, short-legged girl with a face as plain as a pudding.

'Yes,' he answered. 'Oh yes, I am.' Normally he was strict about not speaking to females in public places, but this one had taken him by surprise.

'I love Chopin,' the girl said. She was holding a slim brown paper bag with string handles containing a single record she had just bought. 'I like him better than any of the others.'

It was comforting to hear the voice of this girl after the way the piano salesman had laughed. Mr Botibol wanted to talk to her but he didn't know what to say.

The girl said, 'I like the Nocturnes best, they're so soothing. Which are your favourites?'

Mr Botibol said, 'Well...' The girl looked up at him and she smiled pleasantly, trying to assist him with his embarrassment. It was the smile that did it. He suddenly found himself saying, 'Well now, perhaps, would you, I wonder ... I mean I was wondering...' She smiled again; she couldn't help it this time. 'What I mean is I would be glad if you would care to come along some time and listen to these records.'

'Why how nice of you.' She paused, wondering whether it was all right. 'You really mean it?'

'Yes, I should be glad.'

She had lived long enough in the city to discover that old men, if they are dirty old men, do not bother about trying to pick up a girl as unattractive as herself. Only twice in her life had she been accosted in public and each time the man had been drunk. But this one wasn't drunk. He was nervous and he was peculiar-looking, but he wasn't drunk. Come to think of it, it was she who had started the conversation in the first place. 'It would be lovely,' she said. 'It really would. When could I come?'

Oh dear, Mr Botibol thought. Oh dear, oh dear, oh dear, oh dear.

'I could come tomorrow,' she went on. 'It's my afternoon off.'

'Well, yes, certainly,' he answered slowly. 'Yes, of course. I'll give you my card. Here it is.'

'A. W. Botibol,' she read aloud. 'What a funny name. Mine's Darlington. Miss L. Darlington. How d'you do, Mr Botibol.' She put out her hand for him to shake. 'Oh I *am* looking forward to this! What time shall I come?'

'Any time,' he said. 'Please come any time.'

'Three o'clock?'

'Yes. Three o'clock.'

'Lovely! I'll be there.'

He watched her walk out of the shop, a squat, stumpy, thick-legged little person and my word, he thought, what have I done! He was amazed at himself. But he was not displeased. Then at once he started to worry about whether or not he should let her see his concert-hall. He worried still more when he realized that it was the only place in the house where there was a gramophone.

That evening he had no concert. Instead he sat in his chair brooding about Miss Darlington and what he should do when she arrived. The next morning they brought the piano, a fine Bechstein in dark mahogany which was carried in minus its legs and later assembled on the platform in the concert hall. It was an imposing instrument and when Mr Botibol opened it and pressed a note with his finger, it made no sound at all. He had originally intended to astonish the world with a recital of his first piano compositions – a set of Études – as soon as the piano arrived, but it was no good now. He was too worried about Miss Darlington and three o'clock. At lunch-time his trepidation had increased and he couldn't eat. 'Mason,' he said, 'I'm, I'm expecting a young lady to call at three o'clock.'

'A what, sir?' the butler said.

'A young lady, Mason.'

'Very good, sir.'

'Show her into the sitting-room.'

'Yes, sir.'

Precisely at three he heard the bell ring. A few moments later Mason was showing her into the room. She came in, smiling, and Mr Botibol stood up and shook her hand. 'My!' she exclaimed. 'What a lovely house! I didn't know I was calling on a millionaire!'

She settled her small plump body into a large armchair and

Mr Botibol sat opposite. He didn't know what to say. He felt terrible. But almost at once she began to talk and she chattered away gaily about this and that for a long time without stopping. Mostly it was about his house and the furniture and the carpets and about how nice it was of him to invite her because she didn't have such an awful lot of excitement in her life. She worked hard all day and she shared a room with two other girls in a boarding-house and he could have no idea how thrilling it was for her to be here. Gradually Mr Botibol began to feel better. He sat there listening to the girl, rather liking her, nodding his bald head slowly up and down, and the more she talked, the more he liked her. She was gay and chatty, but underneath all that any fool could see that she was a lonely tired little thing. Even Mr Botibol could see that. He could see it very clearly indeed. It was at this point that he began to play with a daring and risky idea.

'Miss Darlington,' he said. 'I'd like to show you something.' He led her out of the room straight to the little concert-hall. 'Look,' he said.

She stopped just inside the door. 'My goodness! Just look at that! A theatre! A real little theatre!' Then she saw the piano on the platform and the conductor's dais with the brass rail running round it. 'It's for concerts!' she cried. 'Do you really have concerts here! Oh, Mr Botibol, how exciting!'

'Do you like it?'

'Oh yes!'

'Come back into the other room and I'll tell you about it.' Her enthusiasm had given him confidence and he wanted to get going. 'Come back and listen while I tell you something funny.' And when they were seated in the sitting-room again, he began at once to tell her his story. He told the whole thing, right from the beginning, how one day, listening to a symphony, he had imagined himself to be the composer, how he had stood up and started to conduct, how he had got an immense pleasure out of it, how he had done it again with similar results and how finally he had built himself the concert-hall where already he had conducted nine symphonies. But he cheated a little bit in the telling. He said that the only real reason he did it was in order to obtain the maximum appreciation from the music. There was only one way to listen to music, he told her, only one way to make yourself listen to every single note and chord. You had to do two things at once. You had to imagine that you had composed it, and at the same time you had to imagine that the public were hearing it for the first time. 'Do you think,' he said, 'do you really think that any outsider has ever got half as great a thrill from a symphony as the composer himself when he first heard his work played by a full orchestra?'

'No,' she answered timidly. 'Of course not.'

'Then become the composer! Steal his music! Take it away from him and give it to yourself!' He leaned back in his chair and for the first time she saw him smile. He had only just thought of this new complex explanation of his conduct, but to him it seemed a very good one and he smiled. 'Well, what do you think, Miss Darlington?'

'I must say it's very very interesting.' She was polite and puzzled but she was a long way away from him now.

'Would you like to try?'

'Oh no. Please.'

'I wish you would.'

'I'm afraid I don't think I should be able to feel the same way as you do about it, Mr Botibol. I don't think I have a strong enough imagination.'

She could see from his eyes he was disappointed. 'But I'd love to sit in the audience and listen while you do it,' she added.

Then he leapt up from his chair. 'I've got it!' he cried. 'A piano concerto! You play the piano, I conduct. You the greatest pianist, the greatest in the world. First performance of my Piano Concerto No. 1. You playing, me conducting. The greatest pianist and the greatest composer together for the first time. A tremendous occasion! The audience will go mad! There'll be queueing all night outside the hall to get in. It'll be broadcast around the world. It'll, it'll ...' Mr Botibol stopped. He stood behind the chair with both hands resting on the back of the chair and suddenly he looked embarrassed and a trifle sheepish. 'I'm sorry.' he said. 'I get worked up. You see how it is. Even the thought of another performance gets me worked up.'

And then plaintively, 'Would you, Miss Darlington, would you play a piano concerto with me?'

'It's like children,' she said, but she smiled.

'No one will know. No one but us will know anything about it.'

'All right,' she said at last. 'I'll do it. I think I'm daft but just the same I'll do it. It'll be a bit of a lark.'

'Good!' Mr Botibol cried. 'When? Tonight?'

'Oh well, I don't ...'

'Yes,' he said eagerly. 'Please. Make it tonight. Come back and have dinner here with me and we'll give the concert afterwards.' Mr Botibol was excited again now. 'We must make a few plans. Which is your favourite piano concerto, Miss Darlington?'

'Oh well, I should say Beethoven's Emperor.'

'The Emperor it shall be. You will play it tonight. Come to dinner at seven. Evening dress. You must have evening dress for the concert.'

'I've got a dancing dress but I haven't worn it for years.'

'You shall wear it tonight.' He paused and looked at her in silence for a moment; then quite gently, he said, 'You're not worried, Miss Darlington? Perhaps you would rather not do it. I'm afraid, I'm afraid I've let myself get rather carried away. I seem to have pushed you into this. And I know how stupid it must seem to you.'

That's better, she thought. That's much better. Now I know it's all right. 'Oh no,' she said. 'I'm really looking forward to it. But you frightened me a bit, taking it all so seriously.'

When she had gone, he waited for five minutes, then went out into the town to the gramophone shop and bought the records of the Emperor Concerto, conductor, Toscanini - soloist, Horowitz. He turned at once, told his astonished butler that there would be a guest for dinner, then went upstairs and changed into his tails.

She arrived at seven. She was wearing a long sleeveless dress made of some shiny green material and to Mr Botibol she did not look quite so plump or quite so plain as before. He took her straight in to dinner and in spite of the silent disapproving manner in which Mason prowled around the table, the meal went well. She protested gaily when Mr Botibol gave her a second glass of wine, but she didn't refuse it. She chattered away almost without a stop throughout the three courses and Mr Botibol listened and nodded and kept refilling her glass as soon as it was half empty.

Afterwards, when they were seated in the living-room, Mr Botibol said, 'Now Miss Darlington, now we begin to fall into our parts.' The wine, as usual, had made him happy; and the girl, who was even less used to it than the man, was not feeling so bad either. 'You, Miss Darlington, are the great pianist. What is your first name, Miss Darlington?'

'Lucille,' she said.

'The great pianist Lucille Darlington. I am the composer Botibol. We must talk and act and think as though we are pianist and composer.'

'What is *your* first name, Mr Botibol. What does the A stand for?'

'Angel,' he answered.

'Not Angel.'

'Yes,' he said irritably.

'Angel Botibol,' she murmured and she began to giggle. But she checked herself and said, 'I think it's a most unusual and distinguished name.'

'Are you ready, Miss Darlington?'

'Yes.'

Mr Botibol stood up and began pacing nervously up and down the room. He looked at his watch. 'It's nearly time to go on,' he said. 'They tell me the place is packed. Not an empty seat anywhere. I always get nervous before a concert. Do you get nervous, Miss Darlington?'

'Oh yes, I do, always. Especially playing with you.'

'I think they'll like it. I put everything I've got into this concerto, Miss Darlington. It nearly killed me composing it. I was ill for weeks afterwards.'

'Poor you,' she said.

'It's time now,' he said. 'The orchestra are all in their places. Come on.' He led her out and down the passage, then he made her wait outside the door of the concert-hall while he nipped in, arranged the lighting and switched on the gramophone. He came back and fetched her and as they walked on to the stage, the applause broke out. They both stood and bowed towards the darkened auditorium and the applause was vigorous and it went on for a long time. Then Mr Botibol mounted the dais and Miss Darlington took her seat at the piano. The applause died down. Mr Botibol held up his baton. The next record dropped and the Emperor Concerto began.

It was an astonishing affair. The thin stalk-like Mr Botibol, who had no shoulders, standing on the dais in his evening clothes waving his arms about in approximate time to the music; and the plump Miss Darlington in her shiny green dress seated at the keyboard of the enormous piano thumping the silent keys with both hands for all she was worth. She recognized the passages where the piano was meant to be silent, and on these occasions she folded her hands primly on her lap and stared straight ahead with a dreamy and enraptured expression on her face. Watching her, Mr Botibol thought that she was particularly wonderful in the slow solo passages of the Second Movement. She allowed her hands to drift smoothly and gently up and down the keys and she inclined her head first to one side, then to the other, and once she closed her eyes for a long time while she played. During the exciting last movement, Mr Botibol himself lost his balance and would have fallen off the platform had he not saved himself by clutching the brass rail. But in spite of everything, the concerto moved on majestically to its mighty conclusion. Then the real clapping came. Mr Botibol walked over and took Miss Darlington by the hand and led her to the edge of the platform, and there they stood, the two of them, bowing, and bowing, and bowing again as the clapping and the shouting of 'encore' continued. Four times they left the stage and came back, and then, the fifth time, Mr Botibol whispered, 'It's you they want. You take this one alone.' No,' she said. 'It's you. It's you. Please.' But he pushed her forward and she took her call, and came back and said, 'Now you. They want you. Can't you hear them shouting for you.' So Mr Botibol walked alone on to the stage, bowed gravely to right, left and centre and came off just as the clapping stopped altogether.

`He led her straight back to the living-room. He was breathing fast and the sweat was pouring down all over his face. She too was a little breathless, and her cheeks were shining red.

'A tremendous performance, Miss Darlington. Allow me to congratulate you.'

'But what a concerto, Mr Botibol! What a superb concerto!'

'You played it perfectly, Miss Darlington. You have a real feeling for my music.' He was wiping the sweat from his face with a handkerchief. 'And tomorrow we perform my Second Concerto.'

'Tomorrow?'

'Of course. Had you forgotten, Miss Darlington? We are booked to appear together for a whole week.'

'Oh ... oh yes ... I'm afraid I had forgotten that.'

'But it's all right, isn't it?' he asked anxiously. 'After hearing you tonight I could not bear to have anyone else play my music.'

'I think it's all right,' she said. 'Yes, I think that'll be all right.' She looked at the clock on the mantelpiece. 'My heavens, it's late! I must go! I'll never get up in the morning to get to work!'

'To work?' Mr Botibol said. 'To work?' Then slowly, reluctantly, he forced himself back to reality. 'Ah yes, to work. Of course, you have to get to work.'

'I certainly do.'

'Where do you work, Miss Darlington?'

'Me? Well,' and now she hesitated a moment, looking at Mr Botibol. 'As a matter of fact I work at the old Academy.'

'I hope it is pleasant work,' he said. 'What Academy is that?'

'I teach the piano.'

Mr Botibol jumped as though someone had stuck him from behind with a hatpin. His mouth opened very wide.

'It's quite all right,' she said, smiling. 'I've always wanted to be Horowitz. And could I, do you think could I please be Schnabel tomorrow?'

# Vengeance is Mine Inc.

It was snowing when I woke up.

I could tell that it was snowing because there was a kind of brightness in the room and it was quiet outside with no footstep-noises coming up from the street and no tyre-noises but only the engines of the cars. I looked up and I saw George over by the window in his green dressing-gown, bending over the paraffin-stove, making the coffee.

'Snowing,' I said.

'It's cold,' George answered. 'It's really cold.'

I got out of bed and fetched the morning paper from outside the door. It was cold all right and I ran back quickly and jumped into bed and lay still for a while under the bedclothes, holding my hands tight between my legs for warmth.

'No letters?' George said.

'No. No letters.'

'Doesn't look as if the old man's going to cough up.'

'Maybe he thinks four hundred and fifty is enough for one month,' I said.

'He's never been to New York. He doesn't know the cost of living here.'

'You shouldn't have spent it all in one week.'

George stood up and looked at me. '*We* shouldn't have spent it, you mean.'

'That's right,' I said. 'We.' I began reading the paper.

The coffee was ready now and George brought the pot over and put it on the table between our beds. 'A person can't live without money,' he said. 'The old man ought to know that.' He got back into his bed without taking off his green dressing-gown. I went on reading. I finished the racing page and the football page and then I started on Lionel Pantaloon, the great political and society columnist. I always read Pantaloon – same as the other twenty or thirty million people in the

104

country. He's a habit with me; he's more than a habit; he's a part of my morning, like three cups of coffee, or shaving.

'This fellow's got a nerve,' I said.

'Who?'

'This Lionel Pantaloon.'

'What's he saying now?'

'Same sort of thing he's always saying. Same sort of scandal. Always about the rich. Listen to this: "... seen at the Penguin Club ... banker William S. Womberg with beauteous starlet Theresa Williams ... three nights running ... Mrs Womberg at home with a headache ... which is something anyone's wife would have if hubby was out squiring Miss Williams of an evening..."'

'That fixes Womberg,' George said.

'I think it's a shame,' I said. 'That sort of thing could cause a divorce. How can this Pantaloon get away with stuff like that?'

'He always does, they're all scared of him. But if I was William S. Womberg,' George said, 'you know what I'd do? I'd go right out and punch this Lionel Pantaloon right on the nose. Why, that's the only way to handle those guys.'

'Mr Womberg could do that.'

'Why not?'

'Because he's an old man,' I said. 'Mr Womberg is a dignified and respectable old man. He's a very prominent banker in the town. He couldn't possibly...'

And then it happened. Suddenly, from nowhere, the idea came. It came to me right in the middle of what I was saying to George and I stopped short and I could feel the idea itself kind of flowing into my brain and I kept very quiet and let it come and it kept on coming and almost before I knew what had happened I had it all, the whole plan, the whole brilliant magnificent plan worked out clearly in my head; and right then I knew it was a beauty.

I turned and I saw George staring at me with a look of wonder on his face. 'What's wrong?' he said. 'What's the matter?'

I kept quite calm. I reached out and got some more coffee before I allowed myself to speak.

'George,' I said, and I still kept calm. 'I have an idea. Now listen very carefully because I have an idea which will make us both very rich. We are broke, are we not?'

'We are.'

'And this William S. Womberg,' I said, 'would you consider that he is angry with Lionel Pantaloon this morning?'

'Angry!' George shouted. 'Angry! Why, he'll be madder than hell!'

'Quite so. And do you think that he would like to see Lionel Pantaloon receive a good hard punch on the nose?'

'Damn right he would!'

'And now tell me, is it not possible that Mr Womberg would be prepared to pay a sum of money to someone who would undertake to perform this nose-punching operation efficiently and discreetly on his behalf?'

George turned and looked at me, and gently, carefully, he put down his coffee-cup on the table. A slowly widening smile began to spread across his face. 'I get you,' he said. 'I get the idea.'

'That's just a little part of the idea. If you read Pantaloon's column here you will see that there is another person who has been insulted today.' I picked up the paper. 'There is a Mrs Ella Gimple, a prominent socialite who has perhaps a million dollars in the bank . . .'

'What does Pantaloon say about her?'

I looked at the paper again. 'He hints,' I answered, 'at how she makes a stack of money out of her own friends by throwing roulette parties and acting as the bank.'

'That fixes Gimple,' George said. 'And Womberg. Gimple and Womberg.' He was sitting up straight in bed waiting for me to go on.

'Now,' I said, 'we have two different people both loathing Lionel Pantaloon's guts this morning, both wanting desperately to go out and punch him on the nose, and neither of them daring to do it. You understand that?'

'Absolutely.'

'So much then,' I said, 'for Lionel Pantaloon. But don't forget that there are others like him. There are dozens of other columnists who spend their time insulting wealthy and important people. There's Harry Weyman, Claude Taylor, Jacob Swinski, Walter Kennedy, and all the rest of them.'

'That's right,' George said. 'That's absolutely right.'

'I'm telling you, there's nothing that makes the rich so furious as being mocked and insulted in the newspapers.'

'Go on,' George said. 'Go on.'

'All right. Now this is the plan.' I was getting rather excited myself. I was leaning over the side of the bed, resting one hand on the little table, waving the other about in the air as I spoke. 'We will set up immediately an organization and we will call it ... what shall we call it ... we will call it ... let me see ... we will call it "Vengeance Is Mine Inc." ... How about that?'

'Peculiar name.'

'It's biblical. It's good. I like it. "Vengeance Is Mine Inc." It sounds fine. And we will have little cards printed which we will send to all our clients reminding them that they have been insulted and mortified in public and offering to punish the offender in consideration of a sum of money. We will buy all the newspapers and read all the columnists and every day we will send out a dozen or more or our cards to prospective clients.'

'It's marvellous!' George shouted. 'It's terrific!'

'We shall be rich,' I told him. 'We shall be exceedingly wealthy in no time at all.'

'We must start at once!'

I jumped out of bed, fetched a writing-pad and a pencil and ran back to bed again. 'Now,' I said, pulling my knees under the blankets and propping the writing-pad against them, 'the first thing is to decide what we're going to say on the printed cards which we'll be sending to our clients,' and I wrote, 'VENGEANCE IS MINE INC.' as a heading on top of the sheet of paper. Then, with much care, I composed a finely phrased letter explaining the functions of the organization. It finished up with the following sentence: '*Therefore VENGEANCE IS MINE INC. will undertake, on your behalf and in absolute confidence, to administer suitable punishment to columnist*

*.................... and in this regard we respectfully submit to you a choice of methods (together with prices) for your consideration.'*

'What do you mean, "a choice of methods"?' George said.

'We must give them a choice. We must think up a number of things ... a number of different punishments. Number one will be...' and I wrote down, '1. *Punch him one the nose, once, hard.'* 'What shall we charge for that?'

'Five hundred dollars,' George said instantly.

I wrote it down. 'What's the next one?'

'Black his eye,' George said.

I wrote down, '2. *Black his eye ...* $500.'

'No!' George said. 'I disagree with the price. It definitely requires more skill and timing to black an eye nicely than to punch a nose. It is a skilled job. It should be six hundred.'

'O.K.,' I said. 'Six hundred. And what's the next one?'

'Both together, of course. The old one two.' We were in George's territory now. This was right up his street.

'Both together?'

'Absolutely. Punch his nose *and* black his eye. Eleven hundred dollars.'

'There should be a reduction for taking the two,' I said. 'We'll make it a thousand.'

'It's dirt cheap,' George said. 'They'll snap it up.'

'What's next?'

We were both silent now, concentrating fiercely. Three deep parallel grooves of wrinkled skin appeared upon George's rather low sloping forehead. He began to scratch his scalp, slowly but very strongly. I looked away and tried to think of all the terrible things which people had done to other people. Finally I got one, and with George watching the point of my pencil moving over the paper, I wrote: '4. *Put a rattlesnake (with venom extracted) on the floor of his car, by the pedals, when he parks it.'*

'Jesus Christ!' George whispered. 'You want to kill him with fright!'

'Sure,' I said.

'And where'd you get a rattlesnake, anyway?'

'Buy it. You can always buy them. How much shall we charge for that one?'

'Fifteen hundred dollars,' George said firmly. I wrote it down.

'Now we need one more.'

'Here it is,' George said. 'Kidnap him in a car, take all his clothes away except his underpants and his shoes and socks, then dump him out on Fifth Avenue in the rush hour.' He smiled, a broad triumphant smile.

'We can't do that.'

'Write it down. And charge two thousand five hundred bucks. You'd do it all right if old Womberg were to offer you that much.'

'Yes,' I said. 'I suppose I would.' And I wrote it down. 'That's enough now,' I added. 'That gives them a wide choice.'

'And where will we get the cards printed?' George asked.

'George Karnoffsky,' I said. 'Another George. He's a friend of mine. Runs a small printing shop down on Third Avenue. Does wedding invitations and things like that for the big stores. He'll do it. I know he will.'

'Then what are we waiting for?'

We both leapt out of bed and began to dress. 'It's twelve o'clock,' I said. 'If we hurry we'll catch him before he goes to lunch.'

It was still snowing when we went out into the street and the snow was four or five inches thick on the sidewalk, but we covered the fourteen blocks to Karnoffsky's shop at a tremendous pace and we arrived there just as he was putting on his coat to go out.

'Claude!' he shouted. 'Hi boy! How you been keeping,' and he pumped my hand. He had a fat friendly face and a terrible nose with great wide-open nose-wings which overlapped his cheeks by a least an inch on either side. I greeted him and told him that we had come to discuss some most urgent business. He took off his coat and led us back into the office, then I began to tell him about our plans and what we wanted him to do.

When I'd got about quarter way through my story, he

109

started to roar with laughter and it was impossible for me to continue; so I cut it short and handed him the piece of paper with the stuff on it that we wanted him to print. And now, as he read it, his whole body began to shake with laughter and he kept slapping the desk with his hand and coughing and choking and roaring like someone crazy. We sat watching him. We didn't see anything particular to laugh about.

Finally he quietened down and he took out a handkerchief and made a great business about wiping his eyes. 'Never laughed so much,' he said weakly. 'That's a great joke, that is. It's worth a lunch. Come on out and I'll give you lunch.'

'Look,' I said severely, 'this isn't any joke. There is nothing to laugh at. You are witnessing the birth of a new and powerful organization...'

'Come on,' he said and he began to laugh again. 'Come on and have lunch.'

'When can you get those cards printed?' I said. My voice was stern and businesslike.

He paused and stared at us. 'You mean ... you really mean ... you're serious about this thing?'

'Absolutely. You are witnessing the birth...'

'All right,' he said, 'all right,' he stood up. 'I think you're crazy and you'll get in trouble. Sure as hell you'll get in trouble. Those boys like messing other people about, but they don't much fancy being messed about themselves.'

'When can you get them printed, and without any of your workers reading them?'

'For this,' he answered gravely, 'I will give up my lunch. I will set the type myself. It is the least I can do.' He laughed again and the rims of his huge nostrils twitched with pleasure. 'How many do you want?'

'A thousand – to start with, and envelopes.'

'Come back at two o'clock,' he said and I thanked him very much and as we went out we could hear his laughter rumbling down the passage into the back of the shop.

At exactly two o'clock we were back. George Karnoffsky was in his office and the first thing I saw as we went in was the high stack of printed cards on his desk in front of him. They were large cards, about twice the size of ordinary wedding or cocktail invitation-cards. 'There you are,' he said. 'All ready for you.' The fool was still laughing.

He handed us each a card and I examined mine carefully. It was a beautiful thing. He had obviously taken much trouble over it. The card itself was thick and stiff with narrow gold edging all the way around, and the letters of the heading were exceedingly elegant. I cannot reproduce it here in all its splendour, but I can at least show you how it read·

### VENGEANCE IS MINE INC.

Dear ........................

You have probably seen columnist ......................'s slanderous and unprovoked attack upon your character in today's paper. It is an outrageous insinuation, a deliberate distortion of the truth.

Are you yourself prepared to allow this miserable malice-monger to insult you in this manner without doing anything about it?

The whole world knows that it is foreign to the nature of the American people to permit themselves to be insulted either in public or in private without rising up in righteous indignation and demanding – nay, exacting – a just measure of retribution.

On the other hand, it is only natural that a citizen of your standing and reputation will not wish *personally* to become further involved in this sordid petty affair, or indeed to have any *direct* contact whatsoever with this vile person.

How then are you to obtain satisfaction?

The answer is simple. VENGEANCE IS MINE INC. will obtain it for you. We will undertake, on your behalf and in absolute confidence, to administer individual punishment to columnist ............ ........................, and in this regard we respectfully submit to you a choice of methods (together with prices) for your consideration:

1. Punch him on the nose, once, hard    $500
2. Black his eye    $600
3. Punch him on the nose and black his eye    $1000
4. Introduce a rattlesnake (with venom extracted) into his car, on the floor by the pedals, when he parks it    $1500
5. Kidnap him, take all his clothes away except his underpants, his shoes and socks, then dump him out on Fifth Ave. in the rush hour    $2500

This work executed by a professional.

If you desire to avail yourself of any of these offers, kindly reply to VENGEANCE IS MINE INC. at the address indicated upon the enclosed slip of paper. If it is practicable, you will be notified in advance of the place where the action will occur and of the time, so that you may, if you wish, watch the proceedings in person from a safe and anonymous distance.

No payment need be made until after your order has been satisfactorily executed, when an account will be rendered in the usual manner.

George Karnoffsky had done a beautiful job of printing.

'Claude,' he said, 'you like?'

'It's marvellous.'

'It's the best I could do for you. It's like in the war when I would see soldiers going off perhaps to get killed and all the time I would want to be giving them things and doing things for them.' He was beginning to laugh again, so I said, 'We'd better be going now. Have you got large envelopes for these cards?'

'Everything is here. And you can pay me when the money starts coming in.' That seemed to set him off worse than ever and he collapsed into his chair, giggling like a fool. George and I hurried out of the shop into the street, into the cold snow-falling afternoon.

We almost ran the distance back to our room and on the way up I borrowed a Manhattan telephone directory from the public telephone in the hall. We found 'Womberg, William S.' without any trouble and while I read out the address – somewhere up in the East Nineties – George wrote it on one of the envelopes.

'Gimple, Mrs Ella H.' was also in the book and we addressed an envelope to her as well. 'We'll just send to Womberg and Gimple today,' I said. 'We haven't really got started yet. Tomorrow we'll send a dozen.'

'We'd better catch the next post,' George said.

'We'll deliver them by hand,' I told him. 'Now, at once. The sooner they get them the better. Tomorrow might be too late. They won't be half so angry tomorrow as they are today. People are apt to cool off through the night. See here,' I said, 'you go ahead and deliver those two cards right away. While you're doing that I'm going to snoop around the town and try to find out something about the habits of Lionel Pantaloon. See you back here later in the evening...'

At about nine o'clock that evening I returned and found George lying on his bed smoking cigarettes and drinking coffee.

'I delivered them both,' he said. 'Just slipped them through the letter-boxes and rang the bells and beat it up the street. Womberg had a huge house, a huge white house. How did you get on?'

'I went to see a man I know who works in the sports section of the *Daily Mirror*. He told me all.'

'What did he tell you?'

'He said Pantaloon's movements are more or less routine. He operates at night, but wherever he goes earlier in the evening, he *always* – and this is the important point – he *always* finishes up at the Penguin Club. He gets there round about midnight and stays until two or two-thirty. That's when his legmen bring him all the dope.'

'That's all we want to know,' George said happily.

'It's too easy.'

'Money for old rope.'

There was a full bottle of blended whisky in the cupboard and George fetched it out. For the next two hours we sat upon our beds drinking the whisky and making wonderful and complicated plans for the development of our organization. By eleven o'clock we were employing a staff of fifty, including twelve famous pugilists, and our offices were in Rockefeller Center. Towards midnight we had obtained control over all columnists and were dictating their daily columns to them by telephone from our headquarters, taking care to insult and infuriate at least twenty rich persons in one part of the country or another every day. We were immensely wealthy and George had a British Bentley, I had five Cadillacs. George kept practising telephone talks with Lionel Pantaloon. 'That you, Pantaloon?' 'Yes, sir.' 'Well, listen here. I think your column stinks today. It's lousy.' 'I'm very sorry, sir. I'll try to do better tomorrow.' 'Damn right you'll do better, Pantaloon. Matter of

113

fact we've been thinking about getting someone else to take over.' 'But please, please sir, just give me another chance.' 'O.K., Pantaloon, but this is the last. And by the way, the boys are putting a rattlesnake in your car tonight, on behalf of Mr Hiram C. King, the soap manufacturer. Mr King will be watching from across the street so don't forget to act scared when you see it.' 'Yes, sir, of course, sir. I won't forget, sir ...'

When we finally went to bed and the light was out, I could still hear George giving hell to Pantaloon on the telephone.

The next morning we were both woken up by the church clock on the corner striking nine. George got up and went to the door to get the papers and when he came back he was holding a letter in his hand.

'Open it!' I said.

He opened it and carefully he unfolded a single sheet of thin notepaper.

'Read it!' I shouted.

He began to read it aloud, his voice low and serious at first but rising gradually to a high, almost hysterical shout of triumph as the full meaning of the letter was revealed to him. It said:

'*Your methods appear curiously unorthodox. At the same time anything you do to that scoundrel has my approval. So go ahead. Start with Item 1, and if you are successful I'll be only too glad to give you an order to work right on through the list. Send the bill to me. William S. Womberg.*'

I recollect that in the excitement of the moment we did a kind of dance around the room in our pyjamas, praising Mr Womberg in loud voices and singing that we were rich. George turned somesaults on his bed and it is possible that I did the same.

'When shall we do it?' he said. 'Tonight?'

I paused before replying. I refused to be rushed. The pages of history are filled with the names of great men who have come to grief by permitting themselves to make hasty decisions in the excitement of a moment. I put on my dressing-gown, lit a cigarette and began to pace up and down the room. 'There is no hurry,' I said. 'Womberg's order can be dealt with in due course. But first of all we must send out today's cards.'

I dressed quickly, went out to the newsstand across the street, bought one copy of every daily paper there was and returned to our room. The next two hours was spent in reading the columnists' columns, and in the end we had a list of eleven people – eight men and three women – all of whom had been insulted in one way or another by one of the columnists that morning. Things were going well. We were working smoothly. It took us only another half hour to look up the addresses of the insulted ones – two we couldn't find – and to address the envelopes.

In the afternoon we delivered them, and at about six in the evening we got back to our room, tired but triumphant. We made coffee and we fried hamburgers and we had supper in bed. Then we re-read Womberg's letter aloud to each other many many times.

'What he's doing he's giving us an order for six thousand one hundred dollars,' George said. 'Items 1 to 5 inclusive.'

'It's not a bad beginning. Not bad for the first day. Six thousand a day works out at ... let me see ... it's nearly two million dollars a year, not counting Sundays. A million each. It's more than Betty Grable.'

'We are very wealthy people,' George said. He smiled, a slow and wondrous smile of pure contentment.

'In a day or two we will move to a suite of rooms at the St Regis.'

'I think the Waldorf,' George said.

'All right, the Waldorf. And later on we might as well take a house.'

'One like Womberg's?'

'All right. One like Womberg's. But first,' I said, 'we have work to do. Tomorrow we shall deal with Pantaloon. We will catch him as he comes out of the Penguin Club. At two-thirty a.m. we will be waiting for him, and when he comes out into the street you will step forward and you will punch him once, hard, right upon the point of the nose as per contract.'

'It will be a pleasure,' George said. 'It will be a real pleasure. But how do we get away? Do we run?'

'We shall hire a car for an hour. We have just enough money left for that, and I shall be sitting at the wheel with the engine running, not ten yards away, and the door will be open and when you've punched him you'll just jump back into the car and we'll be gone.'

'It is perfect. I shall punch him very hard.' George paused. He clenched his right fist and examined his knuckles. Then he smiled again and he said slowly, 'This nose of his, is it not possible that it will afterwards be so much blunted that it will no longer poke well into other peoples' business?'

'It is quite possible,' I answered, and with that happy thought in our minds we switched out the light and went early to sleep.

The next morning I was woken by a shout and I sat up and saw George standing at the foot of my bed in his pyjamas, waving his arms. 'Look!' he shouted, 'there are four! There are four!' I looked, and indeed there were four letters in his hand.

'Open them. Quickly, open them.'

The first one he read aloud: '"*Dear Vengeance Is Mine Inc., That's the best proposition I've had in years. Go right ahead and give Mr Jacob Swinski the rattlesnake treatment (Item 4). But I'll be glad to pay double if you'll forget to extract the poison from its fangs. Yours Gertrude Porter-Vandervelt. P.S. You'd better insure the snake. That guy's bite carries more poison than any rattler's.*"'.

George read the second one aloud: '"*My cheque for $500 is made out and lies before me on my desk. The moment I receive proof that you have punched Lionel Pantaloon hard on the nose, it will be posted to you. I should prefer a fracture, if possible. Yours etc. Wilbur H. Gollogly.*"'

George read the third one aloud: '"*In my present frame of mind and against my better judgement, I am tempted to reply to your card and to request that you deposit that scoundrel Walter Kennedy upon Fifth Avenue dressed only in his underwear. I make the proviso that there shall be snow upon the ground at the time and that the temperature shall be sub-zero. H. Gresham.*"'

The fourth one also he read aloud: '"*A good hard sock on the nose for Pantaloon is worth five hundred of mine or any-*

*one else's money. I should like to watch. Yours sincerely, Claudia Calthorpe Hines."'*

George laid the letters down gently, carefully upon the bed. For a while there was silence. We stared at each other, too astonished, too happy to speak. I began to calculate the value of those four orders in terms of money.

'That's five thousand dollars worth,' I said softly.

Upon George's face there was a huge bright grin. 'Claude,' he said, 'should we not move now to the Waldorf?'

'Soon,' I answered, 'but at the moment we have no time for moving. We have not even time to send out any fresh cards today. We must start to execute the orders we have in hand. We are overwhelmed with work.'

'Should we not engage extra staff and enlarge our organization?'

'Later,' I said. 'Even for that there is no time today. Just think what we have to do. We have to put a rattlesnake in Jacob Swinski's car ... we have to dump Walter Kennedy on Fifth Avenue in his underpants ... we have to punch Pantaloon on the nose ... let me see ... yes, for three different people we have to punch Pantaloon...'

I stopped. I closed my eyes. I sat still. Again I became conscious of a small clear stream of inspiration flowing into the tissues of my brain. 'I have it!' I shouted. 'I have it! I have it! Three birds with one stone! Three customers with one punch!'

'How?'

'Don't you see? We only need to punch Pantaloon once and each of the three customers ... Womberg, Gollogly and Claudia Hines ... will think it's being done specially for him or her.'

'Say it again.' I said it again.

'It's brilliant.'

'It's common-sense. And the same principle will apply to the others. The rattlesnake treatment and the other one can wait until we have more orders. Perhaps in a few days we shall have ten orders for rattlesnakes in Swinski's car. Then we will do them all in one go.'

'It's wonderful.'

'This evening then,' I said, 'we will handle Pantaloon. But first we must hire a car. Also we must send telegrams, one to Womberg, one to Gollogly and one to Claudia Hines, telling them where and when the punching will take place.'

We dressed rapidly and went out.

In a dirty silent little garage down on East 9th Street we managed to hire a car, a 1934 Chevrolet, eight dollars for the evening. We then sent three telegrams, each one identical and cunningly worded to conceal its true meaning from inquisitive people: *'Hope to see you outside Penguin Club two-thirty a.m. Regards V.I. Mine.'*

'There is one thing more,' I said. 'It is essential that you should be disguised. Pantaloon, or the doorman, for example, must not be able to identify you afterwards. You must wear a false moustache.'

'What about you?'

'Not necessary. I'll be sitting in the car. They won't see me.'

We went to a children's toy-shop and we bought for George a magnificent black moustache, a thing with long pointed ends, waxed and stiff and shining, and when he held it up against his face he looked exactly like the Kaiser of Germany. The man in the shop also sold us a tube of glue and he showed us how the moustache should be attached to the upper lip. 'Going to have fun with the kids?' he asked, and George said, 'Absolutely.'

All was now ready, but there was a long time to wait. We had three dollars left between us and with this we bought a sandwich each and then went to a movie. Then, at eleven o'clock that evening, we collected our car and in it we began to cruise slowly through the streets of New York waiting for the time to pass.

'You're better put on your moustache so as you get used to it.'

We pulled up under a street lamp and I squeezed some glue on to George's upper lip and fixed on the huge black hairy thing with its pointed ends. Then we drove on. It was cold in the car and outside it was beginning to snow again. I could see a few small snowflakes falling through the beams of the car-lights. George kept saying, 'How hard shall I hit him?' and

I kept answering, 'Hit him as hard as you can, and on the nose. It must be on the nose because that is a part of the contract. Everything must be done right. Our clients may be watching.'

At two in the morning we drove slowly past the entrance to the Penguin Club in order to survey the situation. 'I will park there,' I said, 'just past the entrance in that patch of dark. But I will leave the door open for you.'

We drove on. Then George said, 'What does he look like? How do I know it's him?'

'Don't worry,' I answered. 'I've thought of that;' and I took from my pocket a piece of paper and handed it to him. 'You take this and fold it up small and give it to the doorman and tell him to see it gets to Pantaloon quickly. Act as though you are scared to death and in an awful hurry. It's a hundred to one Pantaloon will come out. No columnist could resist that message.'

On the paper I had written: *'I am a worker in Soviet Consulate. Come to the door very quickly please I have something to tell but come quickly as I am in danger. I cannot come in to you.'*

'You see,' I said, 'your moustache will make you look like a Russian. All Russians have big moustaches.'

George took the paper and folded it up very small and held it in his fingers. It was nearly half past two in the morning now and we began to drive towards the Penguin Club.

'You all set?' I said.

'Yes.'

'We're going in now. Here we come. I'll park just past the entrance ... here. Hit him hard,' I said, and George opened the door and got out of the car. I closed the door behind him but I leant over and kept my hand on the handle so I could open it again quick, and I let down the window so I could watch. I kept the engine ticking-over.

I saw George walk swiftly up to the doorman who stood under the red and white canopy which stretched out over the sidewalk. I saw the doorman turn and look down at George and I didn't like the way he did it. He was a tall proud man dressed in a fine magenta-coloured uniform with gold buttons and gold shoulders and a broad white stripe down each magenta trouser-leg. Also he wore white gloves and he stood there looking proudly down at George, frowning, pressing his lips together hard. He was looking at George's moustache and I thought Oh my God we have overdone it. We have over-disguised him. He's going to know it's false and he's going to take one of the long pointed ends in his fingers and then he'll give it a tweak and it'll come off. But he didn't. He was distracted by George's acting, for George was acting well. I could see him hopping about, clasping and unclasping his hands, swaying his body and shaking his head, and I could hear him saying, 'Plees plees plees you must hurry. It is life and teth. Plees plees take it kvick to Mr Pantaloon.' His Russian accent was not like any accent I had heard before, but all the same there was a quality of real despair in his voice.

Finally, gravely, proudly, the doorman said, 'Give me the note.' George gave it to him and said, 'Tank you, tank you, but say it is urgent,' and the doorman disappeared inside. In a few moments he returned and said, 'It's being delivered now.' George paced nervously up and down. I waited, watching the door. Three or four minutes elapsed. George wrung his hands and said, 'Vere is he? Vere is he? Plees to go see if he is not coming!'

'What's the matter with you?' the doorman said. Now he was looking at George's moustache again.

'It is life and teth! Mr Pantaloon can help! He must come!'

'Why don't you shut up,' the doorman said, but he opened the door again and he poked his head inside and I heard him saying something to someone.

To George he said, 'They say he's coming now.'

A moment later the door opened and Pantaloon himself, small and dapper, stepped out. He paused by the door, looking quickly from side to side like a nervous inquisitive ferret. The doorman touched his cap and pointed at George. I heard Pantaloon say, 'Yes, what did you want?'

George said, 'Plees, dis vay a leetle so as novone can hear,' and he led Pantaloon along the pavement, away from the doorman and towards the car.

'Come on, now,' Pantaloon said. 'What is it you want?'

Suddenly George shouted 'Look!' and he pointed up the street. Pantaloon turned his head and as he did so George swung his right arm and he hit Pantaloon plumb on the point of the nose. I saw George leaning forward on the punch, all his weight behind it, and the whole of Pantaloon appeared somehow to lift slightly off the ground and to float backwards for two or three feet until the façade of the Penguin Club stopped him. All this happened very quickly, and then George was in the car beside me and we were off and I could hear the doorman blowing a whistle behind us.

'We've done it!' George gasped. He was excited and out of breath. 'I hit him good! Did you see how good I hit him!'

It was snowing hard now and I drove fast and made many sudden turnings and I knew no one would catch us in this snowstorm.

'Son of a bitch almost went through the wall I hit him so hard.'

'Well done, George,' I said. 'Nice work, George.'

'And did you see him lift? Did you see him lift right up off the ground?'

'Womberg will be pleased,' I said.

'And Gollogly, and the Hines woman.'

'They'll all be pleased,' I said. 'Watch the money coming in.'

'There's a car behind us!' George shouted. 'It's following us! It's right on our tail! Drive like mad!'

'Impossible!' I said. 'They couldn't have picked us up already. It's just another car going somewhere.' I turned sharply to the right.

'He's still with us,' George said. 'Keep turning. We'll lose him soon.'

'How the hell can we lose a police-car in a nineteen thirty-four Chev,' I said. 'I'm going to stop.'

'Keep going!' George shouted. 'You're doing fine.'

'I'm going to stop,' I said. 'It'll only make them mad if we go on.'

George protested fiercely but I knew it was no good and I pulled in to the side of the road. The other car swerved out and went past us and skidded to a standstill in front of us.

'Quick,' George said. 'Let's beat it.' He had the door open and he was ready to run.

'Don't be a fool,' I said. 'Stay where you are. You can't get away now.'

A voice from outside said, 'All right boys, what's the hurry?'

'No hurry,' I answered. 'We're just going home.'

'Yea?'

'Oh yes, we're just on our way home now.'

The man poked his head in through the window on my side, and he looked at me, then at George, then at me again.

'It's a nasty night,' George said. 'We're just trying to reach home before the streets get all snowed up.'

'Well,' the man said, 'you can take it easy. I just thought I'd like to give you this right away.' He dropped a wad of banknotes on to my lap. 'I'm Gollogly,' he added, 'Wilbur H. Gollogly,' and he stood out there in the snow grinning at us, stamping his feet and rubbing his hands to keep them warm. 'I got your wire and I watched the whole thing from across the street. You did a fine job. I'm paying you double. It was worth it. Funniest thing I ever seen. Goodbye boys. Watch your steps. They'll be after you now. Get out of town if I were you. Goodbye.' And before we could say anything, he was gone.

When finally we got back to our room I started packing at once.

'You crazy?' George said. 'We've only got to wait a few hours and we receive five hundred dollars each from Womberg and the Hines woman. Then we'll have two thousand altogether and we can go anywhere we want.'

So we spent the next day waiting in our room and reading the papers, one of which had a whole column on the front page headed, 'Brutal assault on famous columnist'. But sure enough the late afternoon post brought us two letters and there was five hundred dollars in each.

And right now, at this moment, we are sitting in a Pullman car, drinking Scotch whisky and heading south for a place where there is always sunshine and where the horses are running every day. We are immensely wealthy and George keeps saying that if we put the whole of our two thousand dollars on a horse at ten to one we shall make another twenty thousand and we will be able to retire. 'We will have a house at Palm Beach,' he says, 'and we will entertain upon a lavish scale. Beautiful socialites will loll around the edge of our swimming pool sipping cool drinks, and after a while we will perhaps put another large sum of money upon another horse and we shall become wealthier still. Possibly we will become tired of Palm Beach and then we will move around in a leisurely manner among the playgrounds of the rich. Monte Carlo and places like that. Like the Ali Khan and the Duke of Windsor. We will become prominent members of the international set and film stars will smile at us and head-waiters will bow to us and perhaps, in time to come, perhaps we might even get ourselves mentioned in Lionel Pantaloon's column.'

'That would be something,' I said.

'Wouldn't it just,' he answered happily. 'Wouldn't that just be something.'

# The Butler

As soon as George Cleaver had made his first million, he and Mrs Cleaver moved out of their small suburban villa into an elegant London house. They acquired a French chef called Monsieur Estragon and an English butler called Tibbs, both wildly expensive. With the help of these two experts, the Cleavers set out to climb the social ladder and began to give dinner parties several times a week on a lavish scale.

But these dinners never seemed quite to come off. There was no animation, no spark to set the conversation alight, no style at all. Yet the food was superb and the service faultless.

'What the heck's wrong with our parties, Tibbs?' Mr Cleaver said to the butler. 'Why don't nobody never loosen up and let themselves go?'

Tibbs inclined his head to one side and looked at the ceiling. 'I hope, sir, you will not be offended if I offer a small suggestion.'

'What is it?'

'It's the wine, sir.'

'What about the wine?'

'Well, sir, Monsieur Estragon serves superb food. Superb food should be accompanied by superb wine. But you serve them a cheap and very odious Spanish red.'

'Then why in heaven's name didn't you say so before, you twit?' cried Mr Cleaver. 'I'm not short of money. I'll give them the best flipping wine in the world if that's what they want! What *is* the best wine in the world?'

'Claret, sir,' the butler replied, 'from the greatest *châteaux* in Bordeaux – Lafite, Latour, Haut-Brion, Margaux, Mouton-Rothschild and Cheval Blanc. And from only the very greatest vintage years, which are, in my opinion, 1906, 1914, 1929 and 1945. Cheval Blanc was also magnificent in 1895 and 1921, and Haut-Brion in 1906.'

'Buy them all!' said Mr Cleaver. 'Fill the flipping cellar from top to bottom!'

'I can try, sir,' the butler said. 'But wines like these are extremely rare and cost a fortune.'

'I don't give a hoot what they cost!' said Mr Cleaver. 'Just go out and get them!'

That was easier said than done. Nowhere in England or in France could Tibbs find any wine from 1895, 1906, 1914 or 1921. But he did manage to get hold of some twenty-nines and forty-fives. The bills for these wines were astronomical. They were in fact so huge that even Mr Cleaver began to sit up and take notice. And his interest quickly turned into outright enthusiasm when the butler suggested to him that a knowledge of wine was a very considerable social asset. Mr Cleaver bought books on the subject and read them from cover to cover. He also learned a great deal from Tibbs himself, who taught him, among other things, just how wine should properly be tasted. 'First, sir, you sniff it long and deep, with your nose right inside the top of the glass, like this. Then you take a mouthful and you open your lips a tiny bit and suck in air, letting the air bubble through the wine. Watch me do it. Then you roll it vigorously around your mouth. And finally you swallow it.'

In due course, Mr Cleaver came to regard himself as an expert on wine, and inevitably he turned into a colossal bore. 'Ladies and gentlemen,' he would announce at dinner, holding up his glass, 'this is a Margaux '29! The greatest year of the century! Fantastic bouquet! Smells of cowslips! And notice especially the after taste and how the tiny trace of tannin gives it that glorious astringent quality! Terrific, ain't it?'

The guests would nod and sip and mumble a few praises, but that was all.

'What's the matter with the silly twerps?' Mr Cleaver said to Tibbs after this had gone on for some time. 'Don't none of them appreciate a great wine?'

The butler laid his head to one side and gazed upward. 'I think they *would* appreciate it, sir,' he said, 'if they were able to taste it. But they can't.'

'What the heck d'you mean, they can't taste it?'

125

'I believe, sir, that you have instructed Monsieur Estragon to put liberal quantities of vinegar in the salad-dressing.'

'What's wrong with that? I like vinegar.'

'Vinegar,' the butler said, 'is the enemy of wine. It destroys the palate. The dressing should be made of pure olive oil and a little lemon juice. Nothing else.'

'Hogwash!' said Mr Cleaver.

'As you wish, sir.'

'I'll say it again, Tibbs. You're talking hogwash. The vinegar don't spoil my palate one bit.'

'You are very fortunate, sir,' the butler murmured, backing out of the room.

That night at dinner, the host began to mock his butler in front of the guests. 'Mister Tibbs,' he said, 'has been trying to tell me I can't taste my wine if I put vinegar in the salad-dressing. Right, Tibbs?'

'Yes, sir,' Tibbs replied gravely.

'And I told him hogwash. Didn't I, Tibbs?'

'Yes, sir.'

'This wine,' Mr Cleaver went on, raising his glass, 'tastes to me exactly like a Château Lafite '45, and what's more it is a Château Lafite '45.'

Tibbs, the butler, stood very still and erect near the sideboard, his face pale. 'If you'll forgive me, sir,' he said, 'that is not a Lafite '45.'

Mr Cleaver swung round in his chair and stared at the butler. 'What the heck d'you mean,' he said. 'There's the empty bottles beside you to prove it!'

These great clarets, being old and full of sediment, were always decanted by Tibbs before dinner. They were served in cut-glass decanters, while the empty bottles, as is the custom, were placed on the sideboard. Right now, two empty bottles of Lafite '45 were standing on the sideboard for all to see.

'The wine you are drinking, sir,' the butler said quietly, 'happens to be that cheap and rather odious Spanish red.'

Mr Cleaver looked at the wine in his glass, then at the butler. The blood was coming to his face now, his skin was turning scarlet. 'You're lying, Tibbs!' he said.

'No sir, I'm not lying,' the butler said. 'As a matter of fact,

I have never served you any other wine but Spanish red since I've been here. It seemed to suit you very well.'

'Don't believe him!' Mr Cleaver cried out to his guests. 'The man's gone made.'

'Great wines,' the butler said, 'should be treated with reverence. It is bad enough to destroy the palate with three or four cocktails before dinner, as you people do, but when you slosh vinegar over your food into the bargain, then you might just as well be drinking dishwater.'

Ten outraged faces around the table stared at the butler. He had caught them off balance. They were speechless.

'This,' the butler said, reaching out and touching one of the empty bottles lovingly with his fingers, 'this is the last of the forty-fives. The twenty-nines have already been finished. But they were glorious wines. Monsieur Estragon and I enjoyed them immensely.'

The butler bowed and walked quite slowly from the room. He crossed the hall and went out of the front door of the house into the street where Monsieur Estragon was already loading their suitcases into the boot of the small car which they owned together.

### Ah, Sweet Mystery of Life

In this compelling new collection of tales Roald Dahl's urbane wit is directed at the unfathomable mysteries and eccentricities of rural life.

### Kiss Kiss

If your taste is for the macabre, the sick, the outrageous, the unexpected the horrifying – Roald Dahl will give you orgiastic delight. If not, you are going to miss one of the most sophisticated collections of short stories in print.

### Tales of the Unexpected

The stories in this volume (some taken from earlier collections) can stand you on your head, twist you in knots, tie up your hands and leave you gasping for more. Wicked and witty, they lure you into a world as full of unease, coincidence and black humour as you could wish.

### My Uncle Oswald

'Very saucy' – *Daily Express*. 'Deliciously silly' – *Observer*. 'Immense fun!' – *Daily Telegraph*

*and two volumes of autobiography*

### Boy

'Brilliantly coloured, sometimes grotesque and sometimes magical' – *Sunday Times*

### Going Solo

'Very nearly as grotesque as his fiction . . . the same compulsive blend of wide-eyed innocence and fascination with danger and horror' – *Standard*

*Also published*

SOMEONE LIKE YOU
THE WONDERFUL WORLD OF HENRY SUGAR
THE BEST OF ROALD DAHL
OVER TO YOU